Estelle (Körner) Davenport Adams

Sea Song and River Rhyme from Chaucer to Tennyson

Selected and Edited by Estelle Davenport Adams

Estelle (Körner) Davenport Adams

Sea Song and River Rhyme from Chaucer to Tennyson
Selected and Edited by Estelle Davenport Adams

ISBN/EAN: 9783744765336

Printed in Europe, USA, Canada, Australia, Japan

Cover: Foto ©Andreas Hilbeck / pixelio.de

More available books at **www.hansebooks.com**

Sea Song and River Rhyme

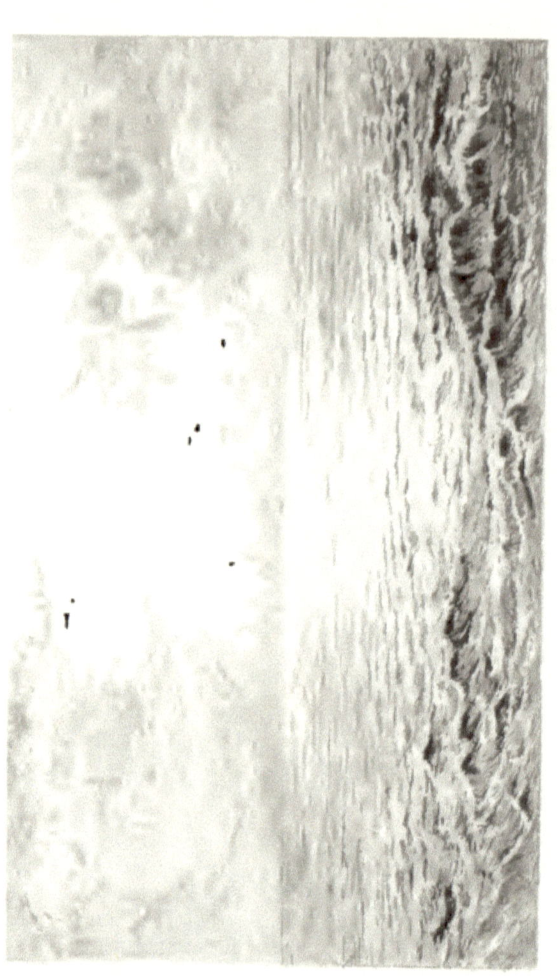

Sea Song
and
River Rhyme

FROM CHAUCER TO TENNYSON

SELECTED AND EDITED BY

ESTELLE DAVENPORT ADAMS

WITH A NEW POEM

BY

ALGERNON CHARLES SWINBURNE

With Twelve Etchings

LONDON
KEGAN PAUL, TRENCH, TRÜBNER & CO. Ltd.
1890

PREFACE.

THIS is a collection of lyrics and passages in English Poetry on the subject of the Sea and Rivers. No attempt has been made to bring together every poetical reference to this topic : for such a purpose a very much larger volume would be required. But the Compiler hopes that none of the most important references have been omitted. She has gone anew through the whole *corpus poetarum*, and has sought to reproduce, wholly or in part, the best of the verse devoted to Stream and Ocean.

Every care has been taken to secure an accurate text, the latest editions being accepted as the authority in the case of living poets, while in that of deceased writers the standard editions have been followed. The arrangement of the letterpress is, as regards deceased authors, chronological ; as regards the living, alphabetical. In general, the songs and extracts are limited to those which deal with the Sea and Rivers as natural objects, and are either descriptive or reflective.

The collection is fortunate in being introduced by a new and important poem from the pen of Mr Swinburne.

The Compiler desires to express her sincere gratitude to those numerous Authors and Publishers who have so kindly permitted her to reproduce pieces of which they hold the copyright. Without their obliging co-operation, she would not have been able to carry out her idea of the volume.

The etchings are the work of Mr Nelson Dawson and Mr W. E. Mackaness.

E. D. A.

A Word for the Navy.

I.

QUEEN born of the sea, that hast borne her
  The mightiest of seamen on earth,
Bright England, whose glories adorn her
  And bid her rejoice in thy birth
    As others made mothers
      Rejoice in births sublime,
    She names thee, she claims thee,
      The lordliest child of time.

II.

All hers is the praise of thy story,
    All thine is the love of her choice :
The light of her waves is thy glory,
    The sound of thy soul is her voice.
        They fear it who hear it
            And love not truth nor thee :
        They sicken, heart-stricken,
            Who see and would not see.

III.

The lords of thy fate, and thy keepers
    Whose charge is the strength of thy ships,
If now they be dreamers and sleepers,
    Or sluggards with lies at their lips,
        Thy haters and traitors,
            False friends or foes descried,
        Might scatter and shatter
            Too soon thy princely pride.

IV.

Smooth France, as a serpent for rancour,
Dark Muscovy, girded with guile,
Lay wait for thee riding at anchor
On waters that whisper and smile.
They deem thee or dream thee
Less living now than dead,
Deep sunken and drunken
With sleep whence fear has fled.

V.

And what though thy song as thine action
Wax faint, and thy place be not known,
While faction is grappling with faction,
Twin curs with thy corpse for a bone?
They care not, who spare not
The noise of pens or throats ;
Who bluster and muster
Blind ranks and bellowing votes.

VI.

Let populace jangle with peerage
 And ministers shuffle their mobs ;
Mad pilots who reck not of steerage
 Though tempest ahead of them throbs.
  That throbbing and sobbing
   Of wind and gradual wave
  They hear not and fear not
   Who guide thee toward thy grave.

VII.

No clamour of cries or of parties
 Is worth but a whisper from thee,
While only the trust of thy heart is
 At one with the soul of the sea.
  In justice her trust is,
   Whose time her tidestreams keep ;
  They sink not, they shrink not,
   Time casts them not on sleep.

VIII.

Sleep thou : for thy past was so royal,
　　Love hardly would bid thee take **heed**
Though France were not constant and loyal
　　Nor Muscovy guiltless of greed.
　　　No nation, in station
　　　　Of story less than thou,
　　　Re-risen from prison,
　　　　Can stand against thee now.

IX.

Sleep on : is the time not a season
　　For strong men to slumber and sleep,
And wise men to palter with **treason ?**
　　And they that sow tares, **shall** they reap ?
　　　The wages of ages
　　　　Wherein men smiled and slept,
　　　Fame fails them, shame veils them,
　　　　Their record is not kept.

X.

Nay, whence is it then that we know it,
  What wages were theirs, and what fame?
Deep voices of prophet and poet
  Bear record against them of shame.
    Death, starker and darker
      Than seals the graveyard grate,
    Entombs them and dooms them
      To darkness deep as fate.

XI.

But thou, though the world should misdoubt thee,
  Be strong as the seas at thy side;
Bind on but thine armour about thee
  That girds thee with power and with pride.
    Where Drake stood, where Blake stood,
      Where fame sees Nelson stand,
    Stand thou too, and now too
      Take thou thy fate in hand.

XII.

At the gate of the sea, in the gateway,
   They stood as the guards of thy gate ;
Take now but thy strengths to thee straightway,
   Though late, we will deem it not late.
    Thy story, thy glory,
      The very soul of thee,
    It rose not, it grows not,
      It comes not save by sea.

ALGERNON CHARLES SWINBURNE.

CONTENTS.

Part 3.—Sea Song.

Contents.

Contents.   xix

Contents.

Contents. xxi

xxii   *Contents.*

Contents.   **xxiii**

Contents.

Part 33.—River-Rhyme.

Contents.   xxix

Part I

SEA SONG

[*From* The Faerie Queene, Book ii., Canto xii.]

WITH that the rolling sea, resounding soft,
　　In his big base them fitly answered;
And on the rocke the waves breaking aloft
A solemne Meane unto them measured.

EDMUND SPENSER.

[*From* King Richard III., Act i., Scene iv.]

LORD, Lord! methought what pain it was to drown!
　　What dreadful noise of water in mine ears!
What ugly sights of death within mine eyes!
Methought I saw a thousand fearful wrecks;
A thousand men that fishes gnaw'd upon;
Wedges of gold, great anchors, heaps of pearl,
Inestimable stones, unvalued jewels,
All scatter'd in the bottom of the sea.
Some lay in dead men's skulls; and in those holes
Where eyes did once inhabit, there were crept,

As 'twere in scorn of eyes, reflecting gems,
That woo'd the slimy bottom of the deep,
And mock'd the dead bones that lay scatter'd by.
            WILLIAM SHAKESPEARE.

[*From* Henry V., Act v., Prologue.]

THE deep-mouth'd sea.
            SHAKESPEARE.

[*From* Julius Cæsar, Act i., Scene iii.]

I HAVE seen
     The ambitious ocean swell and rage and foam,
To be exalted with the threat'ning clouds.
            SHAKESPEARE.

[*From* Taming of the Shrew, Act i., Scene ii.]

HAVE I not heard the sea, puff'd up with winds,
     Rage like an angry boar chafed with sweat?
            SHAKESPEARE.

[*From* Macbeth, Act ii., Scene ii.]

THE multitudinous seas.
            SHAKESPEARE.

[*From* The Tempest, Act i., Scene ii.]

FULL fathom five thy father lies:
    Of his bones are coral made;
Those are pearls that were **his eyes;**
Nothing of him that doth fade
But doth suffer a sea change
Into something rich and strange.
Sea-nymphs hourly ring his knell:
Hark! **now I** hear them,—ding-dong, **bell.**

                       SHAKESPEARE.

[*From* **The Tempest, Act ii., Scene i.**]

I SAW him beat the surges **under him,**
    And ride upon their **backs;** he trod the water,
Whose enmity he **flung aside, and** breasted
The surge most swol'n that met him; his bold **head**
'Bove the contentious waves he kept, and oar'd
Himself with his good arms in lusty stroke
To the shore, that o'er his wave-worn basis bowed,
As stooping to relieve him.

                       SHAKESPEARE.

[*From* **The Tempest, Act v., Scene i.**]

THOUGH the seas threaten, they are merciful.

                       SHAKESPEARE.

[*From* 3 Henry VI., Act ii., Scene v.]

NOW sways it this way, like a mighty sea
    Forc'd by the tide to combat with the wind;
Now sways it that way, like the self-same sea
Forc'd to retire by fury of the wind:
Sometime the flood prevails; and then the wind:
Now one the better; then another best;
Both tugging to be victors, breast to breast,
Yet neither conqueror nor conquered.

SHAKESPEARE.

[*From* Pericles, Act ii., Scene ii.]

THE rough seas, that spare not any man.

SHAKESPEARE.

Safety on the Shore.

WHAT though the sea be calm? Trust to the shore;
    Ships have been drown'd, where late they danc't
    before.

ROBERT HERRICK.

[*From* Battle of the Summer-Islands.]

RUDE seas, that spare not what themselves have nurst.

EDMUND WALLER.

[*From* Paradise Lost, Book vii.]

OVER all the face of Earth
　　Main ocean flowed, not idle, but, with warm
Prolific humour softening all her globe,
Fermented the great mother to conceive,
Satiate with genial moisture ; when God said,
" Be gathered now, ye waters under heaven,
Into one place, and let dry land appear ! "
Immediately the mountains huge appear
Emergent, and their broad bare backs upheave
Into the clouds ; their tops ascend the sky.
So high as heaved the tumid hills, so low
Down sunk a hollow bottom broad and deep,
Capacious bed of waters.　Thither they
Hasted with glad precipitance, uprolled,
As drops on dust conglobing, from the dry :
Part rise in crystal wall, or ridge direct,
For haste ; such flight the great command impressed
On the swift floods.　As armies at the call
Of trumpet (for of armies thou hast heard)
Troop to the standard, so the watery throng,
Wave rolling after wave, where way they found—
If steep, with torrent rapture, if through plain,
Soft-ebbing ; nor withstood them rock or hill ;
But they, or underground, or circuit wide
With serpent error wandering, found their way,
And on the washy ooze deep channels wore :

Easy, ere God had bid the ground be dry,
All but within those banks where rivers now
Stream, and perpetual draw their humid train.
The dry land Earth, and the great receptacle
Of congregated waters he called Seas.

JOHN MILTON.

[*From* Albion and Albanius, Act iii., Scene i.]

Nereids rise out of the Sea, and sing:

FROM the low palace of old father Ocean,
     Come we in pity our cares to deplore ;
Sea-racing dolphins are trained for our motion,
Moony tides swelling to roll us ashore.

Every nymph of the flood, her tresses rending,
Throws off her armlet of pearl in the main ;
Neptune in anguish his charge unattending,
Vessels are foundering, and vows are in vain.

JOHN DRYDEN.

[*From* Song Written at Sea.]

TO all you Ladies now at land
     We men at sea indite ;
But first would have you understand
     How hard it is to write;
The Muses now, and Neptune too,
We must implore to write to you.

For though the Muses should prove kind,
    And fill our empty brain,
Yet if rough Neptune rouse the wind
    To wave the azure main,
Our paper, pen, and ink, and we,
Roll up and down our ships at sea.

Then if we write not by each post,
    Think not we are unkind,
Nor yet conclude our ships are lost
    By Dutchmen, or by wind ;
Our tears we'll send a speedier way,
The tide shall waft them twice a day.

The King, with wonder and surprise,
    Will swear the seas grow bold,
Because the tides will higher rise,
    Than e'er they us'd of old ;
But let him know it is our tears
Bring floods of grief to Whitehall Stairs.
EARL OF DORSET.

[*From* Ocean.]

THE main ! the main !
    Is Britain's reign ;
Her strength, her glory, is her fleet :
    The main ! the main !
    Be Briton's strain ;
As Tritons strong, as Syrens sweet.

Thro' nature wide
Is nought descry'd
So rich in pleasure or surprise ;
When all serene,
How sweet the scene !
How dreadful, when the billows rise,

And storms deface
The fluid glass,
In which erewhile Britannia fair
Look'd down with pride,
Like Ocean's bride,
Adjusting her majestic air !

When tempests cease,
And, hush'd in peace,
The flatten'd surges smoothly spread,
Deep silence keep,
And seem to sleep
Recumbent on their oozy bed ;

With what a trance,
The level glance,
Unbroken, shoots along the seas !
Which tempt from shore
The painted oar ;
And every canvas courts the breeze !

When rushes forth
The frowning North

On black'ning billows, with what dread
   My shuddering soul
   Beholds them roll,
And hears their roarings o'er my head !

   With terror **mark**
   Yon flying bark !
Now centre-deep descend **the brave ;**
   Now, toss'd on high,
   It takes the sky,
A feather on the tow'ring wave !

   Now spins around
   In whirls profound :
Now whelm'd ; now pendant near the clouds ;
   Now stunn'd, it reels
   Midst thunder's peals :
And now fierce lightning **fires the shrouds.**

   All ether burns !
   Chaos returns !
And blends, once more, the seas and skies :
   No space between
   Thy bosom green,
O deep ! and the blue concave, lies.

   The northern blast,
   The shatter'd mast,
The syrt, the whirlpool, and the rock,
   The breaking **spout,**
   The **stars gone out,**
The boiling streight, the monster's shock.

Let others fear ;
To Britain dear
Whate'er promotes her daring claim ;
Those terrors charm,
Which keep her warm
In chase of honest gain, or fame.

EDWARD YOUNG.

[*From* The What d'ye Call It ? Scene viii.]

'TWAS when the seas were roaring
  With hollow blasts of wind ;
A damsel lay deploring,
  All on a rock reclin'd.
Wide o'er the foaming billows
  She cast a wistful look ;
Her head was crown'd with willows
  That tremble o'er the brook.

"Twelve months are gone and over,
  And nine long tedious days.
Why didst thou, vent'rous lover,
  Why didst thou trust the seas ?
Cease, cease, thou cruel ocean,
  And let my lover rest :
Ah ! what's thy troubled motion
  To that within my breast ?

"The merchant, robb'd of pleasure,
  Sees tempest in despair ;

But what's the loss of treasure,
  To losing of my dear?
Should you some coast be laid on
  Where gold and di'monds grow,
You'd find a richer maiden,
  But none that loves you so.

" How can they say that nature
  Has nothing made in vain;
Why, then, beneath the water,
  Should hideous rocks remain?
No eyes the rocks discover
  That lurk beneath the deep,
To wreck the wand'ring lover,
  And leave the maid to weep."

All melancholy lying,
  Thus wail'd she for her dear;
Repay'd each blast with sighing,
  Each billow with a tear;
When o'er the white wave stooping
  His floating corpse she spy'd,
Then, like a lily drooping,
  She bow'd her head, and dy'd.

JOHN GAY.

[*From* The Seasons—Winter.]

THOSE sullen seas,
      That wash'd th' ungenial pole, will rest no more
Beneath the shackles of the mighty north;
But, rousing all their waves, resistless heave.
And hark! the lengthening roar continuous runs
Athwart the rifted deep: at once it bursts,
And piles a thousand mountains to the clouds.
Ill fares the bark with trembling wretches charg'd,
That, tost amid the floating fragments, moors
Beneath the shelter of an icy isle,
While night o'erwhelms the sea, and horror looks
More horrible.   Can human force endure
Th' assembled mischiefs that besiege them round?
Heart-gnawing hunger, fainting weariness,
The roar of winds and waves, the crush of ice,
Now ceasing, now renew'd with louder rage,
And in dire echoes bellowing round the main.
More to embroil the deep, Leviathan
And his unwieldy train, in dreadful sport,
Tempest the loosen'd brine; while, through the gloom,
Far from the bleak inhospitable shore,
Loading the winds, is heard the hungry howl
Of famish'd monsters, there awaiting wrecks.

JAMES THOMSON.

[*From* Hymn to God's Power.]

YE seas, in your eternal roar,
    His sacred praise proclaim;
While the inactive sluggish shore
    Re-echoes to the same.

THOMSON.

[*From* The Shipwreck, Canto iii.]

IN vain the cords and axes were prepared,
    For every wave now smites the quivering yard:
High o'er the ship they throw a dreadful shade,
Then on her burst in terrible cascade;
Across the foundered deck o'erwhelming roar,
And foaming, swelling, bound upon the shore.
Swift up the mountain billow now she flies,
Her shattered top half buried in the skies;
Borne o'er a latent reef the hull impends,
Then thundering on the marble crag descends:
Her ponderous bulk the dire concussion feels,
And o'er upheaving surges wounded reels—
Again she plunges! hark! a second shock
Belges the splitting vessel on the rock—
Down on the vale of death, with dismal cries,
The fated victims shuddering cast their eyes
In wild despair; while yet another stroke
With strong convulsion rends the solid oak:

Ah Heaven !—behold her crashing ribs divide—
She loosens, parts, and spreads in ruin o'er the tide.
WILLIAM FALCONER.

[*From* Retirement.]

OCEAN exhibits, fathomless and broad,
    Much of the power and majesty of God.
He swathes about the swelling of the deep,
That shines, and rests, as infants smile and sleep;
Vast as it is, it answers as it flows
The breathings of the lightest air that blows;
Curling and whitening over all the waste,
The rising waves obey the increasing blast,
Abrupt and horrid as the tempest roars,
Thunder and flash upon the steadfast shores,
Till He that rides the whirlwind checks the rein,
Then all the world of waters sleeps again.
WILLIAM COWPER.

Rondeau.

BLOW high, blow low, let tempests tear
    The main-mast by the board;
My heart, with thoughts of thee, my dear,
    And love, well-stored,

Shall brave all danger, scorn all fear,
  The roaring winds, the raging sea,
    In hopes on shore
    To be once more
Safe **moor'd** with thee.

Alòft while mountains **high we go,**
  The whistling winds **that** scud along,
And the surge **roaring from** below,
    Shall **my signal be**
    To think on thee,
  And this shall be my song :
      Blow high, blow low, let tempests tear
      The main-mast by the board.

And on that night when **all the crew**
  The mem'ry of their former lives
O'er flowing cans of flip renew,
  And drink their sweethearts **and their wives,**
    I'll heave a sigh and **think on thee ;**
    And as the ship rolls through the sea,
    The burthen of my song shall be :
      Blow high, blow low, let tempests tear
     The main-mast by **the board.**

CHARLES DIBDIN.

B

[*From* The Borough, Letter i.]

ALL where the eye delights, yet dreads to roam,
     The breaking billows cast the flying foam
Upon the billows rising—all the deep
Is restless change ; the waves so swell'd and steep,
Breaking and sinking, and the sunken swells,
Nor one, one moment, in its station dwells :
But nearer land you may the billows trace,
As if contending in their watery chase ;
May watch the mightiest till the shoal they reach,
Then break and hurry to their utmost stretch ;
Curl'd as they come, they strike with furious force,
And then, re-flowing, take their grating course,
Raking the rounded flints, which ages past
Roll'd by their rage, and shall to ages last.
    Far off the Petrel in the troubled way
Swims with her brood, or flutters in the spray ;
She rises often, often drops again,
And sports at ease on the tempestuous main.
    High o'er the restless deep, above the reach
Of gunner's hope, vast flocks of Wild-ducks stretch ;
Far as the eye can glance on either side,
In a broad space and level line they glide ;
All in their wedge-like figures from the north,
Day after day, flight after flight, go forth.
    In-shore their passage tribes of Sea-gulls urge,
And drop for prey within the sweeping surge ;
Oft in the rough opposing blast they fly

Far back, then turn and all their force apply,
While to the storm they give their weak complaining cry ;
Or clap the sleek white pinion on the breast,
And in the restless ocean dip for rest.

GEORGE CRABBE.

[*From* The Beacon, Act ii., Scene i.]

NO fish stir in our heaving net,
      And the sky is dark and the night is wet ;
And we must ply the lusty oar,
For the tide is ebbing from the shore ;
And sad are they whose faggots burn,
So kindly stored for our return.

Our boat is small and the tempest raves,
And naught is heard but the lashing waves,
And the sullen roar of the angry sea,
And the wild winds piping drearily ;
Yet sea and tempest rise in vain,
We'll bless our blazing hearths again.

Push bravely, mates !   Our guiding star
Now from its towerlet streameth far,
And now along the nearing strand,
See, swiftly moves yon flaming brand :
Before the midnight watch be past
We'll quaff our bowl and mock the blast.

JOANNA BAILLIE.

[*From* The Sailor.]

THE Sailor sighs as sinks his native shore,
    As all its lessening turrets bluely fade ;
He climbs the mast to feast his eye once more,
And busy fancy fondly lends her aid.

  .   .   .   .

True as the needle, homeward points his heart,
Thro' all the horrors of the stormy main ;
This, the last wish that would with life depart,
To meet the smile of her he loves again.

When Morn first faintly draws her silver line,
Or Eve's grey cloud descends to drink the wave ;
When sea and sky in midnight-darkness join,
Still, still he sees the parting look she gave.

Her gentle spirit, lightly hovering o'er,
Attends his little bark from pole to pole ;
And, when the beating billows round him roar,
Whispers sweet hope to soothe his troubled soul.

  .   .   .   .

But lo, at last he comes with crowded sail !
Lo, o'er the cliff what eager figures bend !
And hark, what mingled murmurs swell the gale !
In each he hears the welcome of a friend.

—'Tis she, 'tis she herself! she waves her hand!
Soon is the anchor cast, the canvas furled;
Soon thro' the whitening surge he springs to land,
And clasps the maid he singled from **the world.**

SAMUEL ROGERS.

[*From* Lines on the View from St Leonards.]

WITH thee beneath my windows, **pleasant** Sea,
    I long not **to** o'erlook earth's **fairest glades**
And green savannahs—Earth has not a plain
So boundless or so **beautiful as** thine;
The eagle's vision cannot take **it in:**
The lightning's wing, **too weak to sweep** its space,
Sinks half-way o'er it **like a wearied bird:**
It is the mirror of the stars, where all
Their hosts within the concave **firmament,**
Gay marching to the music **of the spheres,**
Can see themselves at **once.**

               Nor on the stage
Of rural landscape are there lights and shades
Of more harmonious dance and play than thine.
How vividly this moment brightens forth,
Between grey parallel and leaden breadths,
A belt of hues that stripes thee many a league,
Flush'd like the rainbow, or the ringdove's neck,
And giving to the glancing sea-bird's wing
The semblance of **a meteor.**

                 Mighty Sea!
Cameleon-like thou changest, but there's love
In all thy change, and constant sympathy
With yonder Sky—thy mistress; from her brow
Thou tak'st thy moods and wear'st her colours on
Thy faithful bosom; morning's milky white,
Noon's sapphire, or the saffron glow of eve;
And all thy balmier hours, fair Element,
Have such divine complexion—crisped smiles,
Luxuriant heavings, and sweet whisperings,
That little is the wonder Love's own Queen
From thee of old was fabled to have sprung—
Creation's common! which no human power
Can parcel or inclose; the lordliest floods
And cataracts that the tiny hands of man
Can tame, conduct, or bound, are drops of dew
To thee that could'st subdue the Earth itself,
And brook'st commandment from the heavens alone
For marshalling thy waves.

                Yet, potent Sea!
How placidly thy moist lips speak ev'n now
Along yon sparkling shingles. Who can be
So fanciless as to feel no gratitude
That power and grandeur can be so serene,
Soothing the home-bound navy's peaceful way,
And rocking ev'n the fisher's little bark
As gently as a mother rocks her child?—

.   .   .   .

Old Ocean was

Infinity of ages ere we breathed
Existence—and he will be beautiful
When all the living world **that** sees him now
Shall roll unconscious dust around the sun.
Quelling from **age** to age the vital throb
In human hearts, Death shall **not subjugate**
The pulse that swells in *his* **stupendous** breast,
Or interdict his minstrelsy to sound
In thundering concert with the quiring winds;
But long **as** Man to parent Nature owns
Instinctive homage, and in times beyond
The power of thought to reach, bard after **bard**
Shall sing **thy glory, beatific Sea.**

THOMAS CAMPBELL.

By the Sea-Shore, **Isle of Man.**

WHY stand we gazing on the sparkling Brine,
　　With wonder smit **by its transparency,**
And all-enraptured with its purity?—
Because the unstained, the clear, the crystalline,
Have ever in them something of benign;
Whether **in** gem, in water, or in sky,
A sleeping infant's brow, or wakeful eye
Of a young maiden, only not divine.
Scarcely the hand forbears to dip its palm
For beverage drawn as from a mountain-well.
Temptation centres in the liquid Calm;

Our daily raiment seems no obstacle
To instantaneous plunging in, deep **Sea**!
And revelling in long embrace with thee.

WILLIAM WORDSWORTH.

[*From* On a High Part of the Coast of Cumberland.]

SILENT, and steadfast as the vaulted sky,
   The boundless plain of waters seems to lie :—
Comes that **low sound from** breezes rustling **o'er**
The grass-crowned headland that conceals the shore ?
No ; 'tis the **earth-voice** of the mighty sea,
Whispering how **meek** and gentle he *can* **be** !

WORDSWORTH.

A Sea Piece.

AT nightfall, walking on the **cliff-crown'd** shore,
   Where **sea and sky were in each other** lost ;
Dark ships were scudding through the wild uproar,
Whose wrecks ere morn must strew the dreary coast ;
I mark'd one **well-moor'd** vessel tempest-toss'd,
Sails reef'd, helm lash'd, a dreadful siege she bore,
Her deck by billow after billow cross'd,
While every moment she might be no more :
Yet firmly anchor'd on the nether sand,
Like a chain'd Lion ramping at his foes,
Forward and rearward still she plunged and rose,
Till broke her cable ;—then she fled to land,

With all the waves in chase ; throes following throes ;
She 'scaped,—she struck,—she stood upon the strand

The morn was beautiful, the storm gone by ;
Three days had pass'd ; I saw the peaceful main,
One molten mirror, one illumined plane,
Clear as the blue, sublime, o'erarching sky ;
On shore that lonely vessel caught mine eye,
Her bow was sea-ward, all equipt her train,
Yet to the sun she spread her wings in vain,
Like a chained Eagle, impotent to fly ;
There fix'd as if for ever to abide ;
Far down the beach had roll'd the low neap-tide,
Whose mingling murmur faintly lull'd the ear :
" Is this," methought, "is this the doom of pride,
Check'd in the onset of thy brave career,
Ingloriously to rot by piecemeal here ? "

Spring-tides return'd, and Fortune smiled ; the bay
Received the rushing ocean to its breast ;
While waves on waves innumerably prest,
Seem'd, with the prancing of their proud array,
Sea-horses, flash'd with foam, and snorting spray ;
Their power and thunder broke that vessel's rest ;
Slowly, with new expanding life possest,
To her own element she glid away ;
Buoyant and bounding like the polar Whale,
That takes his pastime ; every joyful sail
Was to the freedom of the wind unfurl'd,
While right and left the parted surges curl'd :

—Go, gallant Bark, with such a tide and gale,
I'll pledge thee to a voyage round the world.

JAMES MONTGOMERY.

[*From* The West Indies, Part i.]

THEN first Columbus, with the mighty hand
    Of grasping genius, weigh'd the sea and land ;
The floods o'erbalanced :—where the tide of light,
Day after day, rolled down the gulph of night,
There seem'd one waste of waters ;—long in vain
His spirit brooded o'er the Atlantic main, ...
Far from the western cliffs he cast his eye
O'er the wide ocean stretching to the sky :
In calm magnificence the sun declined,
And left a paradise of clouds behind :
Proud at his feet, with pomp of pearl and gold
The billows in a sea of glory roll'd.

J. MONTGOMERY.

[*From* Greenland, Canto ii.]

MIGHTY ocean, by whatever name
    Known to vain man, is everywhere the same,
And deems all regions by his gulphs embraced
But vassal tenures of his sovereign waste.

J. MONTGOMERY.

[*From* Greenland, Canto v.]

OCEAN, meanwhile, abroad hath burst the roof
   That sepulchred his waves; he bounds aloof.
In boiling cataracts, as volcanoes spout
Their fiery fountains, gush the waters out; . . . .
         at morn the tempests cease,
And the freed ocean rolls himself to peace;
Broad to the sun his heaving breast expands,
He holds his mirror to a hundred lands.

J. MONTGOMERY.

From A Voyage Round the World.]

EMBLEM of eternity,
   Unbeginning, endless sea!

J. MONTGOMERY.

Song of the Zetland Fisherman.

FAREWELL, merry maidens, to song and to laugh,
   For the brave lads of Westra are bound to the Haaf;
And we must have labour, and hunger, and pain,
Ere we dance with the maids of Dunrossness again.

For now, in our trim boats of Noroway deal,
We must dance on the waves, with the porpoise and seal;
The breeze it shall pipe, so it pipe not too high,
And the gull be our songstress whene'er she flits by.

Sing on, my brave bird, while we follow, like thee,
By bank, shoal, and quicksand, the swarms of the sea ;
And when twenty-score fishes are straining our line,
Sing louder, brave bird, for their spoils shall be thine.

We'll sing while we bait, and we'll sing while we haul,
For the deeps of the Haaf have enough for us all :
There is torsk for the gentle, and skate for the carle,
And there's wealth for bold Magnus, the son of the earl.

Huzza ! my brave comrades, give way for the Haaf,
We shall sooner come back to the dance and the laugh ;
For light without mirth is a lamp without oil ;
Then, mirth and long life to the bold Magnus Troil !

Sir Walter Scott.

[*From* The Lord of the Isles, Canto i.]

FIERCE bounding, forward sprung the ship,
   Like greyhound starting from the slip
    To seize his flying prey.
Awaked before the rushing prow,
The mimic fires of ocean glow,
    Those lightnings of the wave ;
Wild sparkles crest the broken tides,
And, flashing round, the vessel's sides
    With elvish lustre lave,

> While, far behind, their livid light
> To the dark billows of the night
>   A gloomy splendour gave,
> It seems as if old Ocean shakes
> From his dark brow the lucid flakes
>   In envious pageantry,
> To match the meteor-light that streaks
>   Grim Hecla's midnight sky.
>
> Sir W. Scott.

[*From* The Ancient Mariner.]

DOWN dropped the breeze, the sails dropped down,
    'Twas sad as sad could be;
And we did speak only to break
The silence of the sea!

All in a hot and copper sky,
The bloody Sun, at noon,
Right up above the mast did stand,
No bigger than the Moon.

Day after day, day after day
We stuck, nor breath, nor motion;
As idle as a painted ship
Upon a painted ocean.

Water, water, everywhere,
And all the boards did shrink;

Water, water, everywhere,
Nor any drop to drink.

The very deep did rot : O Christ !
That ever this should be !
Yea, slimy things did crawl with legs
Upon the slimy sea.

About, about, in reel and rout
The death-fires danced at night ;
The water, like a witch's oils,
Burned green and blue and white.

SAMUEL TAYLOR COLERIDGE.

[*From* The Stranded Ship.]

HIGH on the beach the ship is stranded,
    And, reft of motion, never more
Must walk above the ocean-roar !
Yet the creatures of the deep, too blest
Within their sunless caves to rest,
In the genial warmth of upper day
Are rolling in unwieldy play,
Or shooting upwards through the light
With arrowy motion silvery bright,
The silent summer air employ
For their region of capricious joy !

While fairy shells in myriads lying,
The smooth hard sand in lustre dyeing,
Encircle **with** a far-seen **chain**
Of glory, the most glorious main !

JAMES HOGG.

[*From* Madoc in Wales.]

The Voyage.

I SAW
  The clouds hang thick and heavy o'er the deep,
And heavily, upon the long slow swell,
The **vessel labour'd on** the labouring sea.
The reef-points rattled on the shivering sail ;
At fits the sudden gust howl'd **ominous,**
Anon with unremitting fury raged ;
High roll'd the mighty **billows, and the blast**
Swept from their sheeted sides the showery foam.
Vain now were all the seamen's homeward hopes,
Vain all their skill ! . . . we drove before the storm.

'Tis pleasant, by the cheerful hearth, to hear
Of tempests and the dangers of the deep,
And pause at times, and feel that we are safe ;
Then listen to the perilous **tale** again,
And with an eager and suspended soul,
Woo terror to delight us. . . . But to hear
The roaring of the raging elements, . . .
To know all human skill, all human strength,

Avail not, . . to look round, and only see
The mountain wave incumbent with its weight
Of bursting waters o'er the reeling bark, . . .
O God, this is indeed a dreadful thing !
And he who hath endured the horror once
Of such an hour, doth never hear the storm
Howl round his home, but he remembers it,
And thinks upon the suffering mariner.

ROBERT SOUTHEY.

[*From* A Triton and Nereid.]

S^O, having moor'd, we lay, like men escaped,
    Idly upon the poop and deck, in talk,
Such as the wanderer loves, . . . Anon, the wave
Was fill'd with wonders, wild and green-hair'd men,
With conchs for trumpets, follow'd by fair nymphs,
That show'd their ivory shoulders through the tide ;
Some, tossing spears of coral, some, pearl crown'd,
And scattering roses—or, with lifted hands,
Reining the purple lips of dolphins yoked,
And huge sea-horses.

                  While we stood amazed ;
A meteor shot above, the trumpets swell'd,
And on a sweeping and high-crested surge,
That stoop'd our pennant to its foaming edge,
Rush'd by two sovereign Shapes, hand twined in hand,
In speechless love !—The waves around were swum

By crowding Cupids, Tritons, **and sweet Nymphs,**
Filling the perfumed air with harmony.

GEORGE CROLY.

An Æstuary.

A Calm Evening.

LOOK on these waters, with how **soft a kiss**
    They woo the pebbled shore **! then steal away,**
Like wanton lovers,—but **to come again,**
And die in music !—**There,** the bending skies
See all their **stars,—and the** beach-loving trees,
Osiers and willows, **and** the watery flowers,
That wreathe their **pale roots round the ancient stones,**
Make pictures of themselves !

G. CROLY.

[*From* **The Ground Swell.**]

HOW soft the shades of evening creep
    O'er yonder dewy lea,
Where balmy winds have lull'd to sleep
  The tenants of the tree.
No wandering breeze is here to sweep,
In shadowy ripple o'er the deep,
  Yet swells the heaving sea !

How calm the **sky !** rest, ocean, **rest,**
  From storm and ruffle free,

Calm as the image on thy breast
    Of her that governs thee !
And yet beneath the moon's mild **reign**
  Thy broad breast heaves as one **in pain,**
    Thou dark and silent **sea.**

REGINALD HEBER.

[*From* The Isle of Palms, Canto i.]

IT is the midnight hour :—the beauteous Sea,
  Calm as **the** cloudless heaven, the heaven discloses,
While many **a sparkling star, in** quiet **glee,**
Far down within **the** watery sky reposes.
As if the Ocean's **heart** were stirred
With inward life, **a sound is heard,**
Like that **of dreamer** murmuring **in his sleep ;**
'Tis partly the billow, and partly the **air**
That lies like a garment floating **fair**
Above the happy deep.
The sea, I ween, cannot be fanned
By evening freshness **from the land,**
For the land it **is far away ;**
But God hath willed that the **sky-born** breeze
In the centre of the loneliest **seas**
Should ever sport and play.

   .   .   .   .   .   .

She mocketh that gentle Mighty **One**
As he lies in his quiet mood.
" Art thou," she breathes, **"the** Tyrant grim

That scoffest at human prayers,
Answering with prouder roar the while,
As it rises from some lonely isle,
Through groans raised wild, the hopeless hymn
Of shipwrecked mariners?
Oh! thou art harmless as a child
Weary with joy, and reconciled
For sleep to change its play;
And now that night hath stayed thy race,
Smiles wander o'er thy placid face
As if thy dreams were gay!"

PROFESSOR WILSON.

The Sea-Cliffs of Kilkee.

AWFULLY beautiful art thou, O sea!
   Viewed from the vantage of these giant rocks,
  That vast in air lift their primeval blocks,
Screening the sandy cove of lone Kilkee.
Cautious, with outstretched arm, and bended knee,
  I scan the dread abyss, 'till the depth mocks
  My straining eyeballs, and the eternal shocks
Of billows rolling from infinity
Disturb my brain. Hark! the shrill sea-birds' scream!
  Cloud-like they sweep the long wave's sapphire gleam,
  Ere the poised Osprey stoop in wrath from high.
Here man, alone, is naught; Nature supreme,
  Where all is simply great that meets the eye—
  The precipice, the ocean, and the sky.

SIR AUBREY DE VERE.

[*From* Malby Sands.]

YON sea, like a tired warrior,
    For quiet joy hath laid aside his power.

SIR A. DE VERE.

[*From* Childe Harold's Pilgrimage, Canto iii.]

ONCE more upon the waters! yet once more!
    And the waves bound beneath me as a steed
That knows his rider.   Welcome to their roar!
Swift be their guidance, wheresoe'er it lead!
Though the strain'd mast should quiver as a reed,
And the rent canvas fluttering strew the gale,
Still must I on; for I am as a weed,
Flung from the rock, on Ocean's foam to sail
Where'er the surge may sweep, the tempest's breath prevail.

GEORGE, LORD BYRON.

[*From* Childe Harold's Pilgrimage, Canto iv.]

ROLL on, thou deep and dark blue Ocean—roll!
    Ten thousand fleets sweep over thee in vain;
Man marks the earth with ruin—his control
Stops with the shore; upon the watery plain
The wrecks are all thy deed, nor doth remain
A shadow of man's ravage, save his own,
When, for a moment, like a drop of rain,

He sinks into thy depths with bubbling groan,
Without a grave, unknell'd, uncoffin'd, and unknown.

His steps are not upon thy paths,—thy fields
Are not a spoil for him,—thou dost arise
And shake him from thee ; the vile strength he wields
For earth's destruction thou dost all despise,
Spurning him from thy bosom to the skies,
And send'st him, shivering in thy playful spray
And howling, to his Gods, where haply lies
His petty hope in some near port or bay,
And dashest him again to earth :—there let him lay.

The armaments which thunderstrike the walls
Of rock-built cities, bidding nations quake
And monarchs tremble in their capitals,
The oak leviathans, whose huge ribs make
Their clay creator the vain title take
Of lord of thee, and arbiter of war—
These are thy toys, and, as the snowy flake,
They melt into thy yeast of waves, which mar
Alike the Armada's pride or spoils of Trafalgar.

Thy shores are empires, changed in all save thee—
Assyria, Greece, Rome, Carthage, what are they ?
Thy waters wash'd them power while they were free,
And many a tyrant since ; their shores obey
The stranger, slave, or savage ; their decay
Has dried up realms to deserts :—not so thou ;—
Unchangeable, save to thy wild waves' play,

Time writes no wrinkle **on** thine azure brow :
Such as creation's dawn beheld, thou rollest now.

Thou glorious mirror, where the Almighty's form
Glasses **itself in tempests ; in** all **time,—**
Calm or convulsed, **in breeze,** or gale, **or storm,**
Icing the pole, or **in the torrid clime**
Dark-heaving—boundless, endless, and **sublime,**
The image of eternity, **the throne**
Of the Invisible ; even from out thy slime
The monsters of the deep are made ; each **zone**
Obeys thee ; thou goest forth, dread, fathomless, **alone.**

And **I have loved thee, Ocean** ! and my joy
Of youthful **sports was on thy** breast to be
Borne, like **thy bubbles, onward : from** a **boy**
I wanton'd **with thy breakers—they to me**
Were **a** delight **; and if the freshening sea**
Made them a terror—'twas **a pleasing fear,**
For I was as it were **a** child of thee,
And trusted to thy **billows** far and near,
And laid my hand upon **thy** mane—as **I** do here.

BYRON.

[*From* Childe Harold's Pilgrimage, Canto iv.]

THERE **is** a rapture on the lonely shore,
    There is society, where none intrudes,
By the deep Sea, and music in **its roar.**

BYRON.

[*From* Don Juan, Canto ii.]

THE vast, salt, dread, eternal deep.

BYRON.

[*From* The Siege of Corinth.]

THERE shrinks no ebb in that tideless sea,
    Which changeless rolls eternally.

BYRON.

[*From* The Fall of Jerusalem.]

ON the margin of the flood
    With lifted rod the Prophet stood;
And the summon'd east wind blew,
And aside it sternly threw
The gather'd waves, that took their stand,
Like crystal rocks, on either hand,
Or walls of sea-green marble piled
Round some irregular city wild.

Then the light of morning lay
On the wonder-pavèd way,
Where the treasures of the deep
In their caves of coral sleep.
The profound abysses, where
Was never sound from upper air,

Rang with Israel's chanted **words** :
King of kings ! and Lord of lords !

Then with bow and banner glancing,
  On exulting Egypt came,
With her chosen horsemen prancing,
  And her cars on wheels of flame,
In a rich and boastful ring
All around her furious king.

But the Lord from **out His cloud,**
The Lord look'd down upon the proud ;
And the host drave heavily
Down the deep bosom of the sea.

With a quick and sudden **swell,**
Prone the liquid **ramparts** fell ;
Over horse, and over **car,**
Over every man of war,
Over Pharaoh's crown **of gold,**
The loud thundering **billows roll'd.**
As the level waters spread,
Down they sank, they sank like lead,
Down without a cry or groan.
And the morning sun, that shone
On myriads of bright-armed men,
Its meridian radiance then
Cast on a wide sea, heaving, as **of yore,**
Against a silent, solitary shore.

HENRY HART MILMAN.

[*From* To Jane—The Recollection.]

WE wandered to the pine forest
   That skirts the ocean's foam ;
The lightest wind was in its nest,
   The tempest in its home.
The whispering waves were half asleep,
   The clouds were gone to play,
And on the bosom of the deep,
   The smile of Heaven lay ;
It seemed as if the hour were one
   Sent from beyond the skies,
Which scattered from above the sun
   A light of paradise.

PERCY BYSSHE SHELLEY.

Time.

UNFATHOMABLE Sea ! whose waves are years !
   Ocean of Time, whose waters of deep woe
Are brackish with the salt of human tears !
   Thou shoreless flood which in thy ebb and flow
Claspest the limits of mortality,
And, sick of prey, yet howling on for more,
Vomitest thy wrecks on its inhospitable shore !
Treacherous in calm, and terrible in storm,
   Who shall put forth on thee,
   Unfathomable sea ?

SHELLEY.

[*From* Stanzas written in Dejection.]

I SEE the deep's untrampled floor,
   With green and purple sea-weeds strown;
I see the waves upon the shore,
   Like light dissolved, in star-showers thrown.
   I sit upon the sands alone,
The lightning of the noontide ocean
   Is flashing round me, and a tone
Arises from its measured motion—
How sweet, did any heart now share in my emotion !

SHELLEY.

[*From* The Revolt of Islam, Canto i.]

THE evening was most clear
   And beautiful; and there the sea I found,
Calm as a cradled child in dreamless slumber bound.

SHELLEY.

[*From* Second Sunday after Trinity.]

WHEN up some woodland dale we catch
   The many-twinkling smile of ocean,
Or with pleas'd ear bewilder'd watch
   His chime of restless motion;

Still as the surging waves retire,
They seem to gasp with strong desire,
Such signs of love old Ocean gives,
We cannot choose but think he lives.

JOHN KEBLE.

The Ocean.

HE that in venturous barks hath been
    A wanderer on the deep,
Can tell of many an awful scene,
    Where storms for ever sweep.

For many a fair, majestic sight
    Hath met his wandering eye,
Beneath the streaming northern light,
    Or blaze of Indian sky.

Go ! ask him of the whirlpool's roar,
    Whose echoing thunder peals
Loud, as if rush'd along the shore
    An army's chariot-wheels ;

Of icebergs, floating o'er the main,
    Or fixed upon the coast,
Like glittering citadel or fane,
    Mid the bright realms of frost ;

Of coral rocks from waves below
    In steep ascent that tower,

And, fraught with peril, daily grow,
   Form'd by an insect's power;

Of sea-fires, which at dead of night
   Shine o'er the tides afar,
And make the expanse of ocean bright,
   As heaven with many a star.

O God ! Thy name *they* well may praise
   Who to the deep go down,
And trace the wonders of thy ways
   Where rocks and billows frown !

If glorious be that awful deep
   No human power can bind,
What then art *Thou*, who bid'st it keep
   Within its bounds confined !

Let heaven and earth in praise unite !
   Eternal praise to Thee,
Whose word can rouse the tempest's might,
   Or still the raging sea !

Felicia Dorothea Hemans.

The Treasures of the Deep.

WHAT hidest thou in thy treasure-caves and cells,
   Thou hollow-sounding and mysterious main?
Pale glistening pearls, and rainbow-coloured shells,
   Bright things which gleam unrecked of and in vain !—

Keep, keep thy riches, melancholy **sea** !
      We ask not such from thee.

Yet more, the depths have more !—What wealth untold,
   Far down, and shining through their stillness lies !
Thou hast the starry gems, the burning gold,
   Won from ten thousand **royal** argosies !—
Sweep o'er thy spoils, thou wild **and wrathful main** !
      Earth claims not *these* again.

Yet more, the depths have **more** ! **Thy waves have** rolled
   Above the cities of **a world** gone **by** !
Sand hath filled up **the** palaces of **old,**
   Sea-weed **o'ergrown** the halls of revelry—
Dash o'er them, **ocean! in thy scornful** play !
      Man **yields them to decay.**

Yet more ! the billows and the **depths have more !**
   High hearts and brave are gathered to thy breast !
They hear not now the booming waters roar,
   The battle-thunders will not break their rest—
Keep thy red gold and gems, thou stormy grave !
      Give back the **true** and brave !

Give back the lost and lovely !—those for whom
   The place **was** kept at board and hearth so long !
The prayer went up through midnight's breathless gloom,
   And the vain yearning woke 'midst festal song !
Hold fast thy buried isles, thy towers o'erthrown—
      But all is not thine own.

To thee the love of woman hath gone down,
  Dark flow thy tides o'er manhood's noble head,
O'er youth's bright locks, and beauty's flowery crown !
  Yet must thou hear a voice—Restore the dead !
Earth shall reclaim her precious things from thee !—
        Restore the dead, thou sea !

F. D. HEMANS.

A Thought of the Sea.

MY earliest memories to thy shores are bound,
  Thy solemn shores, thou ever-chanting main !
The first rich sunsets, kindling thought profound
In my lone being, made thy restless plain
As the vast, shining floor of some dread fane,
All paved with glass and fire.   Yet, O blue deep !
Thou that no trace of human hearts dost keep,
Never to thee did love with silvery chain
Draw my soul's dream, which through all nature sought
What waves deny,—some bower of *steadfast* bliss,
A *home* to twine with fancy, feeling, thought,
As with sweet flowers :—But chasten'd hope for this
Now turns from earth's green valleys, as from thee,
To that sole changeless world, where " there is no more sea."

F. D. HEMANS.

Distant Sound of the Sea at Evening.

YET, rolling far up some green mountain-dale,
    Oft let me hear, as ofttimes I have heard,
Thy swell, thou deep ! when evening calls the bird
And bee to rest; when summer tints grow pale,
Seen through the gathering of a dewy veil;
And peasant-steps are hastening to repose,
And gleaming flocks lie down, and flower-cups close
To the last whisper of the falling gale.
Then, midst the dying of all other sound,
When the Soul hears thy distant voice profound,
Lone-worshipping, and knows that through the night
'Twill worship still, then most its anthem-tone
Speaks to our being of the Eternal One,
Who girds tired nature with unslumbering might.

F. D. HEMANS.

A Hymn of the Sea.

THE sea is mighty, but a mightier sways
    His restless billows. Thou, whose hands have scooped
His boundless gulfs and built his shore, thy breath,
That moved in the beginning o'er his face
Moves o'er it evermore.   The obedient waves
To its strong motion roll, and rise and fall.
Still from that realm of rain thy cloud goes up,
As at the first, to water the great earth,

And keep her valleys green.   A hundred realms
Watch its broad shadow warping on the wind,
And in the drooping shower, with gladness hear
Thy promise of the harvest.   I look forth
Over the boundless blue, where joyously
The bright crests of innumerable waves
Glance to the sun at once, as when the hands
Of a great multitude are upward flung
In acclamation.   I behold the ships
Gliding from cape to cape, from isle to isle,
Or stemming toward far lands, or hastening home
From the Old World.   It is thy friendly breeze
That bears them, with the riches of the land,
And treasure of dear lives, till, in the port,
The shouting seamen climbs and furls the sail.

　But who shall bide thy tempest, who shall face
The blast that wakes the fury of the sea?
O God! Thy justice makes the world turn pale,
When on the armèd fleet, that royally
Bears down the surges, carrying war, to smite
Some city, or invade some thoughtless realm,
Descends the fierce tornado.   The vast hulks
Are whirled like chaff upon the waves ; the sails
Fly, rent like webs of gossamer ; the masts
Are snapped asunder ; downward from the decks,
Downward are slung, into the fathomless gulf,
Their cruel engines , and their hosts, arrayed
In trappings of the battlefield are whelmed
By whirlpools, or dashed dead upon the rocks.

Then stand the nations still with awe, and pause,
A moment, from the bloody work of war.

  These restless surges eat away the shores
Of earth's old continents ; the fertile plain
Welters in shallows, headlands crumble down,
And the tide drifts the sea-sand in the streets
Of the drowned city.   Thou, meanwhile, afar
In the green chambers of the middle sea,
Where broadest spread the waters and the line
Sinks deepest, while no eye beholds thy work.
Creator ! thou dost teach the coral-worm
To lay his mighty reefs.   From age to age
He builds beneath the waters, till, at last,
His bulwarks overtop the brine, and check
The long wave rolling from the southern pole
To break upon Japan.   Thou bidd'st the fires,
That smoulder under ocean, heave on high
The new-made mountains, and uplift their peaks,
A place of refuge for the storm-driven bird.
The birds and wafting billows plant the rifts
With herb and tree ; sweet fountains gush ; sweet airs
Ripple the living lakes that, fringed with flowers,
Are gathered in the hollows.   Thou dost look
On thy creation and pronounce it good.
Its valleys, glorious in their summer green,
Praise thee in silent beauty, and its woods,
Swept by the murmuring winds of ocean, join
The murmuring shores in a perpetual hymn.

WILLIAM CULLEN BRYANT.

D

[*From* Thanatopsis.]

OLD Ocean's gray and melancholy waste.

W. C. BRYANT.

[*From* Endymion, Book i.]

THE surgy murmurs of the lonely sea.

JOHN KEATS.

[*From* Endymion, Book ii.]

AS when heaved anew
   Old ocean rolls a lengthen'd wave to the shore,
Down whose green back the short-lived foam, all hoar,
Bursts gradual, with a wayward indolence.

KEATS.

[*From* A Reminiscence of Claude's Enchanted
Castle.]

THE rocks were silent, the wide sea did weave
   An untumultuous fringe of silver foam
Along the flat brown sand.

KEATS.

Sonnet XI.

HOW long I sail'd, and never took a thought
    To what port I was bound! Secure as sleep,
I dwelt upon the bosom of the deep
And perilous sea.   And though my ship was fraught
With rare and precious fancies, jewels brought
From fairy-land, no course I cared to keep,
Nor changeful wind nor tide I heeded ought,
But joy'd to feel the merry billows leap,
And watch the sunbeams dallying with the waves;
Or haply dream what realms beneath may lie
Where the clear ocean is an emerald sky,
And mermaids warble in their coral caves,
Yet vainly woo me to their secret home;
And sweet it were for ever so to roam.

HARTLEY COLERIDGE.

Song of the Danish Sea-King.

OUR bark is on the waters deep, our bright blades in
    our hand,
Our birthright is the ocean vast—we scorn the girdled land;
And the hollow wind is our music brave, and none can
    bolder be,
Than the hoarse-tongued tempest raving o'er a proud and
    swelling sea!

Our bark is dancing on the waves, its tall masts quivering
  bend
Before the gale, which hails us now with the hollo of a
  friend ;
And its prow is sheering merrily the upcurl'd billow's foam,
While our hearts, with throbbing gladness, cheer old Ocean
  as our home !

Our eagle-wings of might we stretch before the gallant wind,
And we leave the tame and sluggish earth a dim, mean
  speck behind ;
We shoot into the untrack'd deep, as earth-freed spirits soar,
Like stars of fire through boundless space—through realms
  without a shore !

Lords of this wide-spread wilderness of waters, we bound free,
The haughty elements alone dispute our sovereignty ;
No landmark doth our freedom let, for no law of man can
  mete
The sky which arches o'er our head—the waves which kiss
  our feet !

The warrior of the land may back the wild horse, in his
  pride ;
But a fiercer steed we dauntless breast—the untamed ocean
  tide ;
And a nobler tilt our bark careers, as it quells the saucy
  wave,
While the Herald storm peals o'er the deep the glories of
  the brave.

Hurrah ! hurrah ! the wind is up—it bloweth fresh and free,
And every cord, instinct with life, pipes loud its fearless
    glee ;
Big swell the bosom'd sails with joy, and they madly kiss
    the spray,
As proudly, through the foaming surge, the Sea-King bears
    away !

WILLIAM MOTHERWELL.

[*From* Love, and Home, and Native Land.]

WHEN o'er the silent deep we rove,
    More fondly then our thoughts will stray
To those we leave —to those we love,
    Whose prayers pursue our wat'ry way.
When in the lonely midnight hour
    The sailor takes his watchful stand,
His heart then feels the holiest power
    Of love, and home, and native land.

SAMUEL LOVER.

On a Naval Officer buried in the Atlantic.

THERE is, in the wide, lone sea,
    A spot unmarked, but holy,
For there the gallant and the free
    In his ocean bed lies lowly.

Down, down, beneath the deep,
  That oft to triumph bore him,
He sleeps a sound and pleasant sleep,
  With the salt waves washing o'er him.

He sleeps serene, and safe
  From tempest or from billow;
Where the storms that high above him chafe
  Scarce rock his peaceful pillow.

The sea and him in death
  They did not dare to sever;
It was his home while he had breath,
  'Tis now his home for ever.

Sleep on thou mighty dead!
  A glorious tomb they've found thee;
The broad blue sky above thee spread,
  The boundless waters round thee.

No vulgar foot treads here,
  No hand profane shall move thee,
But gallant fleets shall proudly steer,
  And warriors shout, above thee.

And when the last trump shall sound
  And tombs are asunder riven,
Like the morning sun from the wave thou'lt bound,
  To rise and shine in heaven.

HENRY FRANCIS LYTE.

The Sea.

THE Sea ! the Sea ! the open Sea !
   The blue, the fresh, the ever free !
Without a mark, without a bound,
It runneth the earth's wide regions round ;
It plays with the clouds ; it mocks the skies ;
Or like a cradled creature lies.

I'm on the Sea ! I'm on the Sea !
I am where I would ever be !
With the blue above, and the blue below,
And silence wheresoe'er I go ;
If a storm should come and awake the deep,
What matter ? *I* shall ride and sleep.

I love (oh, *how* I love) to ride
On the fierce foaming, bursting tide,
When every mad wave drowns the moon.
Or whistles aloft his tempest tune,
And tells how goeth the world below,
And why the south-west blasts do blow.

I never was on the dull, tame shore,
But I lov'd the great Sea more and more,
And backwards flew to her billowy breast,
Like a bird that seeketh its mother's nest—
And a mother she *was* and *is* to me,
For I was born on the open Sea !

The waves were white, and red the morn,
In the noisy hour when I was born ;
And the whale it whistled, the porpoise rolled,
And the dolphins bared their backs of gold ;
And never was heard such an outcry wild,
As welcomed to life the Ocean child !

I've lived since then, in calm and strife,
Full fifty summers a sailor's life,
With wealth to spend and a power to range,
But never have sought nor sighed for change ;
And Death, whenever he comes to me,
Shall come on the wild unbounded Sea !

BRYAN WALLER PROCTER.

The Stormy Petrel.

A THOUSAND miles from land are we,
  Tossing about on the roaring sea ;
From billow to bounding billow cast,
Like fleecy snow on the stormy blast :
The sails are scattered abroad like weeds ;
The strong masts shake, like quivering reeds ;
The mighty cables and iron chains,
The hull, which all earthly strength disdains,
They strain, and they crack ; and hearts like stone
Their natural, hard, proud strength disown.

Up and down ! up and down !
From the base of the wave to the billow's crown

And amidst the flashing and feathery foam,
The Stormy Petrel finds a home—
A home, if such a place may be,
For her who lives on the wide, wide sea,
On the craggy ice, in the frozen air,
And only seeketh her rocky lair
To warm her young, and to teach them spring
At once o'er the wave on their stormy wing !

O'er the Deep ! o'er the Deep !
Where the whale, and the shark, and the sword-fish sleep,
Outflying the blast and the driving rain,
The Petrel telleth her tale—in vain ;
For the mariner curseth the warning bird,
Who bringeth him news of the storms unheard !
—Ah ! thus does the prophet, of good or ill,
Meet hate from the creatures he serveth still !
Yet *he* ne'er falters :—so, Petrel, spring
Once more o'er the waves on thy stormy wing !

B. W. PROCTER.

The Sea—in Calm.

LOOK what immortal floods the sunset pours
    Upon us—Mark ! how still (as though in dreams
Bound) the once wild and terrible Ocean seems !
How silent are the winds ! no billow roars ;
But all is tranquil as Elysian shores !

The silver margin which aye runneth round
The moon-enchanted sea, hath here no sound ;
Even Echo speaks not on these radiant moors !

What ! is the Giant of the ocean dead,
Whose strength was all unmatch'd beneath the sun ?
No : he reposes ! Now his toils are done ;
More quiet than the babbling brooks is he.
So mightiest powers by deepest calms are fed,
And sleep, how oft, in things that gentlest be !

B. W. Procter.

[*From* Marcian Colonna, Part iii.]

O THOU vast Ocean ! Ever-sounding Sea !
    Thou symbol of a drear immensity !
Thou thing that windest round the solid world
Like a huge animal, which, downward hurl'd
From the black clouds, lies weltering and alone,
Lashing and writhing till its strength be gone.
Thy voice is like the thunder, and thy sleep
Is as a giant's slumber, loud and deep.
Thou speakest in the East and in the West
At once, and on thy heavily-laden breast
Fleets come and go, and shapes that have no life
Or motion, yet are moved and meet in strife. . .
—Thou only, terrible Ocean, hast a power,
A will, a voice, and in thy wrathful hour,
When thou dost lift thine anger to the clouds,
A fearful and magnificent beauty shrouds

Thy broad green forehead.   If thy waves be driven
Backwards and forwards by the shifting wind,
How quickly dost thou thy great strength unbind,
And stretch thine arms, and war at once with Heaven.

Thou trackless and immeasurable Main !
On thee no record ever lived again
To meet the hand that writ it : line nor lead
Hath ever fathomed thy profoundest deeps,
Where haply the huge monster swells and sleeps,
King of his watery limit, who 'tis said
Can move the mighty ocean into storm—
Oh ! wonderful thou art, great element :
And fearful in thy spleeny humours bent,
And lovely in repose ; thy summer form
Is beautiful, and when thy silver waves
Make music in earth's dark and winding caves,
I love to wander on thy pebbled beach,
Marking the sunlight at the evening hour,
And hearken to the thoughts thy waters teach—
" Eternity, Eternity, and Power."

B. W. PROCTER.

[*From* The Course of Time, Book vii.]

GREAT Ocean ! strongest of creation's sons,
    Unconquerable, unreposed, untired ;
That roll'd the wild, profound, eternal bass,
In Nature's anthem, and made music, such

As pleased the ear of God !   Original,
Unmarr'd, unfaded work of Deity ;
And unburlesqued by mortal's puny skill.
From age to age, enduring and unchanged :
Majestical, inimitable, vast,
Loud uttering satire day and night on each
Succeeding race, and little pompous work
Of man.   Unfallen, religious, holy sea !
Thou bow'dst thy glorious head to none, fear'dst none,
Heard'st none, to none did'st honour, but to God
Thy Maker—only worthy to receive
Thy great obeisance.   Undiscover'd sea !
Into thy dark, unknown, mysterious caves,
And secret haunts, unfathomably deep
Beneath all visible retired, none went,
And came again, to tell the wonders there.
Tremendous Sea ! what time thou lifted up
Thy waves on high, and with thy winds and storms
Strange pastime took, and shook thy mighty sides
Indignantly,—the pride of navies fell ;
Beyond the arm of help, unheard, unseen,
Sunk friend and foe, with all their wealth and war ;
And on thy shores, men of a thousand tribes,
Polite and barbarous, trembling stood, amazed,
Confounded, terrified, and thought vast thoughts
Of ruin, boundlessness, omnipotence,
Infinitude, eternity ; and thought
And wonder'd still, and grasp'd and grasp'd and grasp'd
Again ; beyond her reach exerting all
The soul to take thy great idea in,

To comprehend incomprehensible ;
And wonder'd more, and felt their littleness.
Self-purifying, unpolluted Sea !
Lover unchangeable ! thy faithful breast
For ever heaving to the lovely moon,
That like a shy and holy virgin, **robed**
In saintly white, walk'd nightly **in the heavens,**
And to the everlasting serenade
Gave gracious audience, **nor was woo'd in vain.**

ROBERT POLLOK.

[*From* The Course of Time, Book iv.]

H E [Byron] laid his hand upon **"the Ocean's mane,"**
And played familiar with **his hoary locks.**

POLLOK.

[*From* The Child of the Sea.]

I T was a summer evening; and **the sea**
Seem'd to rejoice in its tranquillity ;
Rolling its gentle **waters to** the **west,**
Till the rich **crimson blush'd** upon their breast,
Uniting lovingly **the wave** and sky,
Like Hope **content** in its delight to die.

LETITIA ELIZABETH LANDON.

[*From* As o'er the Deep the Seaman Roves.]

AS o'er the deep the seaman roves
 With cloud and storm above him,
Far, far from all the smiles he loves,
 And all the hearts that love him,
'Tis sweet to find some friendly mast
 O'er that same ocean sailing,
And listen in the hollow blast
 To hear the pilot's hailing.

On rolls the sea ! and brief the bliss,
 And farewell follows greeting ;
On rolls the sea ! one hour is his
 For parting and for meeting ;
And who shall tell, on sea or shore,
 In sorrow or in laughter,
If he shall see that vessel more,
 Or hear that voice hereafter ?

     WILLIAM MACKWORTH PRAED.

[*From* Death's Jest Book, Act i.]

TO sea to sea !   The calm is o'er ;
 The wanton water leaps in sport,
And rattles down the pebbly shore ;
 The dolphin wheels, the sea-cows snort,
And unseen mermaid's pearly song
Comes bubbling up, the weeds among.

Fling broad the sail, dip deep the oar:
To sea, to sea! the calm is o'er.

To sea, to sea! our wide-winged bark
  Shall billowy cleave its sunny way,
And with its shadow, fleet and dark,
  Break the caved Tritons' azure day,
  Like mighty eagle soaring light
O'er antelopes on Alpine height.
  The anchor heaves, the ship swings free,
  The sails swell full.   To sea, to sea!
THOMAS LOVELL BEDDOES.

[*From* Wood Notes, ii.]

THE sea tosses and foams to find
  Its way up to the cloud and wind.
RALPH WALDO EMERSON.

[*From* King Arthur, Book ix.]

A LONELY ship—lone in the measureless sea,
    Lone in the channel thro' the frozen steeps,
Like some bold thought launch'd on infinity
  By early sage—comes glimmering up the deeps!
The dull wave, dirge-like, moans beneath the oar;
The dull air heaves with wings that glide before.

.   .   .   .

Crash'd thro' the dreary air a thunder peal !
  In their slow courses meet two ice-rock isles
Clanging ; the wide seas far-resounding reel ;
  The toppling ruin rolls in the defiles ;
The pent tides quicken with the headlong shock ;
Broad-billowing heave the long waves from the rock ;

Far down the booming vales precipitous
  Plunges the stricken galley,—as a steed
Smit by the shaft runs reinless,—o'er the prows
  Howl the lash'd surges ; man and monster freed
By power more awful from the savage fray,
Here roaring sink—there dumbly whirl away.

The water runs in mäelstroms,—as a reed
  Spins in an eddy and then skirs along,—
Dragg'd round and round, emerged and vanishëd
  The mighty ship amidst the mightier throng
Of the revolving hell.   With abrupt spring
Bounding at last—on it shot maddening.

Behind it, thunderous swept the glacier masses,
  Shivering and splintering, hurtling each on each :
Narrower and narrower press the frowning passes :—
  Jamm'd in the farthest gorge the bark may reach,
Where the grim Scylla locks the direful way,
The fierce Charybdis flings her mangled prey.

As if a living thing, in very part
  The vessel groans—and with a dismal chime

Cracks to the cracking ice ; asunder start
  The brazen ribs :—and, clogg'd and freezing, climb
Thro' cleft and chink, as thro' their native caves,
The gelid armies of the hardening waves.
          EDWARD, LORD LYTTON.

[*From* The Image on the Tide.]

THE sense cannot count
    (As the waters glass
The forest and mount
    And the clouds that pass)

The shadows and gleams
    In that stilly deep,
Like the tranquil dreams
    Of a hermit's sleep.
          LORD LYTTON.

[*From* Travels of Theodore Elbert.]

ONCE more, thou darkly rolling main,
  I bid thy lonely strength adieu ;
And sorrowing leave thee once again,
  Familiar long, yet ever new !

.   .   .   .   .   .

Thy many voices, which are one,
   The varying garbs that robe thy might,
Thy dazzling hues at set of sun,
   Thy deeper loveliness by night;

The shades that flit with every breeze
   Along thy hoar and agèd brow,—
What has the universe like these,
   Or what so strong, so fair as thou?

JOHN STERLING.

The Tide rises, the Tide falls.

THE tide rises, the tide falls,
   The twilight darkens, the curlew calls;
Along the sea-sands damp and brown
The traveller hastens toward the town,
   And the tide rises, the tide falls.

Darkness settles on roofs and walls,
But the sea in the darkness calls and calls;
The little waves, with their soft, white hands,
Efface the footprints in the sands,
   And the tide rises, the tide falls.

The morning breaks; the steeds in their stalls
Stamp and neigh, as the hostler calls;
The day returns, but never more
Returns the traveller to the shore,
   And the tide rises, the tide falls.

HENRY WADSWORTH LONGFELLOW

The City and the Sea.

THE panting City cried to the Sea,
   "I am faint with heat,—O breathe on me!"

And the Sea said, "Lo, I breathe! but my breath
To some will be life, to others death!"

As to Prometheus, bringing ease
In pain, come the Oceanides,

So to the City, hot with the flame
Of the pitiless sun, the east wind came.

It came from the heaving breast of the deep,
Silent as dreams are, and sudden as sleep.

Life-giving, death-giving, which will it be;
O breath of the merciful, merciless Sea?

H. W. LONGFELLOW.

The Sound of the Sea.

THE sea awoke at midnight from its sleep,
   And round the pebbly beaches far and wide
I heard the first wave of the rising tide
Rush onward with uninterrupted sweep;
A voice out of the silence of the deep,
   A sound mysteriously multiplied

As of a cataract from the mountain's side,
　Or roar of winds upon a wooded steep.
So comes to us at times, from the unknown
　And inaccessible solitudes of being,
　The rushing of the sea-tides of the soul ;
And inspirations that we deem our own
　Are one divine foreshadowing and foreseeing
　Of things beyond our reason and control.

　　　　　　　　　　　H. W. Longfellow.

[*From* Sea-Weed.]

WHEN descends on the Atlantic
　　　　The gigantic
Storm-wind of the equinox,
Landward in his wrath he scourges
　The toiling surges,
Laden with sea-weed from the rocks :

From Bermuda's reefs ; from edges
　Of sunken ledges,
In some far-off, bright Azore ;
From Bahama, and the dashing,
　Silver-flashing
Surges of San Salvador ;

From the tumbling surf, that buries
　The Orkneyan skerries,
Answering the hoarse Hebrides ;

And from wrecks of ships, and drifting
  Spars, uplifting
On the desolate, rainy seas ;—

Ever drifting, drifting, drifting
  On the shifting
Currents of the restless main ;
Till in sheltered coves, and reaches
  Of sandy beaches,
All have found repose again.

H. W. LONGFELLOW.

[*From* The Secret of the Sea.]

HE heard the ancient helmsman
  Chant a song so wild and clear,
That the sailing sea-bird slowly
  Poised upon the mast to hear,

Till his soul was full of longing,
  And he cried, with impulse strong,—
" Helmsman ! for the love of heaven,
  Teach me, too, that wondrous song !"

" Would'st thou,"—so the helmsman answered,
  " Learn the secret of the sea?
Only those who brave its dangers
  Comprehend its mystery !"

H. W. LONGFELLOW.

[*From* Evangeline, Introduction.]

LOUD from its rocky caverns, the deep-voiced neigh-
    bouring ocean
Speaks, and in accents disconsolate **answers the wail** of the
    forest.

H. W. Longfellow.

[*From* Evangeline, Part i.]

AND in haste the refluent ocean
    Fled **away from the shore, and left the line of** the
    sand-beach
Covered with waifs of the **tide, with kelp and the slippery**
    sea-weed. . . .
Back to its nethermost caves retreated the bellowing ocean,
Dragging **adown the** beach the rattling pebbles, and leaving
Inland and far up the shore the stranded boats of the sailors.

H. W. Longfellow.

[*From* Evangeline, Part i.]

AND as **the** voice **of the priest** repeated **the service of**
    sorrow,
Lo ! **with a mournful sound,** like the voice **of a vast con-**
    gregation,
Solemnly answered the sea, and mingled its **roar** with the
    dirges.

'Twas the returning tide, that afar from the waste of the
    ocean,
With the first dawn of the day, came heaving and hurrying
    landward.

H. W. LONGFELLOW.

[*From* Twilight.]

LIKE the wings of sea-birds
    Flash the white caps of the sea.

H. W. LONGFELLOW.

[*From* The Saga of King Olaf, xiv.]

THE waters vast
    Filled them with a vague devotion,
With the freedom and the motion,
With the roll and roar of ocean
    And the sounding blast.

H. W. LONGFELLOW.

[*From* Four by the Clock.]

THE heavy breathing of the sea
    Is the only sound that comes to me.

H. W. LONGFELLOW.

[*From* The Courtship of Miles Standish, iv.]

LIKE an awakened conscience, the sea was moaning
  and tossing,
Beating remorseful and loud the mutable sands of the sea-
 shore.

        H. W. LONGFELLOW.

[*From* The Building of the Ship.]

THAT awful, pitiless sea,
  With all its terror and mystery,
The dim, dark sea, so like unto death,
That divides and yet unites mankind !

        H. W. LONGFELLOW.

The Ocean.

THE ocean, at the bidding of the Moon,
  For ever changes with his restless tide ;
Flung shoreward now, to be regather'd soon
With kingly pauses of reluctant pride,
And semblance of return. Anon from home
He issues forth again, high ridged and free ;
The seething hiss of his tumultuous foam,
Like armies whispering where great echoes be ?
Oh ! leave me here upon this beach to rove,

Mute **listener** to that sound **so grand and lone—**
A glorious sound, deep drawn and strongly thrown,
And reaching those on mountain heights above ;
To British ears, as who shall scorn to own,
A tutelar fond voice, a Saviour-tone of love !

CHARLES TENNYSON **TURNER.**

The Quiet Tide near Ardrossan.

ON to the beach the quiet waters crept :
    But, though I stood not far within the land,
No tidal murmur reach'd me from the strand.
The mirror'd clouds beneath old Arran slept.
I look'd again across the watery waste :
The shores **were** full, the **tide was near** its height,
Though scarcely heard **: the reefs were** drowning fast,
And an imperial whisper told the might
Of the outer floods, that press'd into the bay,
Though **all** besides was silent. **I** delight
In the rough billows, and the foam-ball's flight :
I love the shore upon a stormy day ;
But yet more stately were the power **and ease**
That with **a** whisper deepen'd **all the seas.**

C. T. TURNER.

[*From* Aurora Leigh, Book iii.]

THE sea, that blue end of the world,
　That fair scroll-finis of a wicked book.
　　　　　　ELIZABETH BARRETT BROWNING.

[*From* Aurora Leigh, Book vii.]

AND lo, the city of Marseilles,
　With all her ships behind her, and beyond,
The scimitar of ever-shining sea,
For right-hand use, bared blue against the sky !
　　　　　　E. B. BROWNING.

[*From* The Soul's Travelling.]

MIGHTY Sea,
　Can we dwarf thy magnitude
And fit it to our straitest mood?
　　　　　　E. B. BROWNING.

[*From* a Sea-side Walk.]

AND shining with a gloom, the water grey
　Swang in its moon-taught way.
　　　　　　E. B. BROWNING.

[*From* A Sabbath Morning at Sea.]

TOO strait ye are, capacious **seas,**
  To satisfy the **loving !**

                        E. B. BROWNING.

[*From* Written in Edinburgh.]

AND the broad sea beyond, in calm or rage,
  Chainless alike, **and teaching Liberty.**

                        ARTHUR HENRY HALLAM.

[*From* At Venice.]

WHEN the proud sea, for Venice' sake,
  Itself consents **to wear**
The semblance of a land-locked lake,
Inviolably fair ;
And in the dalliance of **her Isles,**
Has levelled his strong waves,
Adoring her with tenderer wiles,
Than his own pearly caves,—

Surely may *we* to similar calm,
Our noisy lives subdue,
And bare our bosoms **to** such balm
As God **has given to few :**

Surely may we delight to pause
On our care-goaded road,
Refuged from Time's most bitter laws
In this august abode.

RICHARD, LORD HOUGHTON.

[*From* The Lay of the Humble.]

I DO remember well, when first
   I saw the great blue sea,—
It was no stranger-face, that burst
In terror upon me;
My heart began, from the first glance,
His solemn pulse to follow,
I danced with every billow's dance,
And shouted to their hollo.

LORD HOUGHTON.

[*From* The Eld.]

I SAW the hoary bulk of ocean
   A'couching on the shore,
With a ripple for its motion,
   And a murmur for its roar.

LORD HOUGHTON.

[*From* Songs in Absence.]

I.

COME home, come home ! and where is home for me,
    Whose ship is driving o'er the trackless sea ?
To the frail bark here plunging on its way,
To the wild waters, shall **I turn and say**
To the plunging bark, or to the **salt sea foam,**
    You are my home.

Fields once I walked in, **faces once** I knew,
Familiar things so old my heart believed **them true,**
These far, far back, behind me lie, **before**
The dark clouds mutter, and **the deep seas roar,**
And speak to them that 'neath and **o'er them roam**
    No words of home.

Beyond the clouds, **beyond the** waves that roar,
There may indeed, **or may not be, a shore,**
Where fields as green, **and** hands **and hearts as true,**
The old forgotten semblance may renew,
And offer exiles driven far **o'er** the salt sea foam,
    Another home.

    .   .   .   .   .

Come home, come home ! and where a home **hath** he
Whose ship **is** driving o'er the driving sea ?
Through **clouds** that mutter, and o'er waves that roar,
Say shall we find, or shall we not, a shore
That is, as is not ship or ocean foam,
    Indeed our home ?

ARTHUR HUGH CLOUGH.

II.

COME back, come back, behold with straining mast
  And swelling sail, behold her steaming fast;
With one new sun to see her voyage o'er,
With morning light to touch her native shore.
  Come back, come back.

Come back, come back, while westward labouring by,
With sail-less yards, a bare black hulk we fly.
See how the gale we fight with, sweeps her back,
To our lost home, on our forsaken track.
  Come back, come back.

 .   .   .   .   .

Come back, come back, more eager than the breeze,
The flying fancies sweep across the seas,
And lighter far than ocean's flying foam,
The heart's fond message hurries to its home.
  Come back, come back.

Come back, come back !
Back flies the foam; the hoisted flag streams back;
The long smoke wavers on the homeward track,
Back fly with winds things which the winds obey,
The strong ship follows its appointed way.

        A. H. CLOUGH

III.

WHERE lies the land to which the ship would go
  Far, far ahead, is all her seamen know.
And where the land she travels from? Away,
Far, far behind, is all that they can say.

On sunny noons upon the deck's smooth face,
Linked arm in arm, how pleasant here to pace ;
Or, o'er the stern reclining, watch **below**
The foaming wake far widening as we **go.**

On stormy nights when wild north-westers rave,
How proud a thing to fight with wind and wave !
The dripping sailor on the reeling mast
Exults to bear, and scorns to wish it **past.**

Where lies the land to which the ship would go?
Far, far ahead, is all **her seamen know.**
And where the land she **travels from?   Away,**
Far, far behind, is all that they can say.

A. H. Clough.

The Sands of Dee.

"O MARY, go and **call the cattle home,**
      And call **the cattle home,**
    And call the cattle home
  Across the sands of Dee ;"
The western wind **was wild** and dank with **foam,**
  And all alone **went she.**

The **western** tide crept up along the sand,
      And o'er and o'er the sand,
      And round and round the sand,
    As far as eyes could see.

The rolling **mist came** down and hid the **land** :
    And never home came she.

"**Oh** ! **is it weed, or fish, or floating hair**—
    A tress of golden hair,
    A drownèd maiden's hair,
    Above the nets at sea?
Was never salmon yet that shone so **fair**
    Among the stakes on Dee."

They rowed her in across the rolling foam,
    The cruel crawling foam,
    The cruel hungry foam,
    To her grave beside the sea :
But still the boatmen hear her call the **cattle home**
    Across the sands of Dee.

Charles Kingsley.

[*From* Andromeda.]

ONWARD they came in their **joy, and around them the**
    lamps of the sea-nymphs,
Myriad fiery globes, swam panting and heaving ; and rain-
    bows,
Crimson and azure and emerald, were broken in star-
    showers, lighting
Far through **the wine-dark depths of the crystal, the gardens**
    of Nereus,

Coral and sea-fan and tangle, the blooms and the palms of
    the ocean.
  Onward they came in their joy, more white than the foam
    which they scattered,
Laughing and singing and tossing and twining, while eager,
    the Tritons
Blinded with kisses their eyes, unreproved, and above them
    in worship
Hovered the terns, and the sea-gulls swept past them on
    silvery pinions,
Echoing softly their laughter; around them the wantoning
    dolphins
Sighed as they plunged, full of love; and the great sea-
    horses which bore them
Curved up their crests in their pride to the delicate arms
    of the maidens,
Pawing the spray into gems, till a fiery rainfall, unharming,
Sparkled and gleamed on the limbs of the nymphs, and the
    coils of the mermen.
  Onward they went in their joy, bathed round with the
    fiery coolness,
Needing nor sun nor moon, self-lighted, immortal: but others,
Pitiful, floated in silence apart; in their bosoms the sea-
    boys,
Slain by the wrath of the seas, swept down by the anger of
    Nereus;
Hapless, whom never again on strand or on quay shall
    their mothers
Welcome with garlands and vows to the temple, but wearily
    pining,

F

Gaze over island and bay for the sails of the sunken ; they
  heedless
Sleep in soft bosoms for ever, and dream of the surge and
  the sea-maids.

         C. KINGSLEY.

[*From* The Spanish Gipsy, Book i.]

THE Mid Sea that moans with memories.

         GEORGE ELIOT.

[*From* The Spanish Gipsy, Book i.]

THE untravelled ocean's restless tides.

         GEORGE ELIOT.

[*From* The Spanish Gipsy, Book iv.]

PUSH off the boat,
  Quit, quit the shore,
    The stars will guide us back :—
O gathering cloud,
  O wide, wide sea,
    O waves that keep no track !

         GEORGE ELIOT.

[*From* A Minor Prophet.]

THE sense of vastness, when **at night**
    We hear the roll and **dash** of **waves that break**
Nearer and nearer with the rushing tide,
Which rises to the level of the cliff
Because the wide Atlantic **rolls** behind
Throbbing respondent to the far-off orbs.

GEORGE ELIOT.

[*From* Home at last.]

FEAR not, my child !
    Though the waves are white and high,
And the storm blows wild
    Through the gloomy sky ;
On the edge of the western **sea,**
    See that line of golden light,
    Is the haven bright
Where home is awaiting thee ;
    Where, this **peril past,**
We shall rest from **our stormy voyage**
    In peace at last.

    Be not afraid ;
But give me thy hand, and see
    How the waves have made
    A cradle for thee.

Night is come, dear, and we shall rest ;
So turn **from** the angry skies,
And close thine eyes,
And lay thy head on my **breast** :
Child, do not weep ;
In the calm, cold, purple depths
There we shall sleep.

ADELAIDE ANNE PROCTER.

[*From* Unexpressed.]

WAVES of an unfathomable sea.

A. A. PROCTER.

[*From* A Legend of Provence.]

ALL still, all silent, save the sobbing **rush**
Of rippling waves, that lapsed in silver hush
Upon the beach ; where, glittering towards the strand,
The purple Mediterranean kissed **the** land.

A. A. PROCTER.

The Sea-Limits.

CONSIDER the sea's listless chime ;
Time's self it is, **made** audible,—
The murmur of the **earth's** own shell.

Secret continuance sublime
   Is the sea's end : our sight may pass
   No furlong **further.   Since time was,**
This sound hath told the lapse of time.

No quiet, **which** is death's,—it **hath**
   The mournfulness of ancient life,
   Enduring always at dull **strife.**
As the world's heart of rest and wrath,
   Its painful pulse is in the sands.
   Last utterly, the whole sky stands,
Grey and not known, **along** its path.

Listen alone besides the sea,
   Listen alone among the woods ;
   Those voices of twin solitudes
Shall have one sound alike to thee :
   Hark where the murmurs of thronged men
   Surge and sink back and surge again,—
Still the one voice of wave and tree.

Gather a shell from the strown **beach**
   And listen at its lips : they sigh
   The same desire and mystery,
The echo of the whole sea's speech.
   And all mankind is thus at heart
   Not anything but what thou art :
And Earth, Sea, Man, are all in each.

DANTE GABRIEL ROSSETTI.

[*From* The Wine of Circe.]

TO-NIGHT shall echo back the unchanging roar
    Which sounds for ever from the tide-strown shore
Where the dishevelled sea-weed hates the sea.

D. G. ROSSETTI.

[*From* The Portrait.]

UPON the desolate verge of light
    Yearned loud the iron-bosomed sea.

D. G. ROSSETTI.

[*From* Sonnet.]

ALTHOUGH its heart is rich in pearls and ores,
    The sea complains upon a thousand shores.

ALEXANDER SMITH.

[*From* The Music of the Sea.]

I HAVE not seen the glorious sea
    Since I was a little child,
Ocean-bred in a fisher's hut,
    Wash'd by the waters wild.

And now the shells upon my shelf
  Are dearer than aught to me !
My soul still longs and listens for
  The music of **the sea.**

I learnt to **walk to the sound of the waves,**
  The **shingly beach along;**
The salt-spray dashed **against the pane,**
  That was my cradle-song.
The sea-mew's cry was far before
  The thrushes' song to me,
O ! my heart still longs and listens for
  The music **of** the sea.

To drag nets full of gleaming fish,
  Under the silver moon ;
To watch ships on the far blue line,
  Grow nearer in the noon ;
To make friends with the storm, instead
  Of a city's din for me ;—
My heart longs wearily to **hear**
  The music of the sea !

HAMILTON AÏDÉ.

[*From To* ——.]

THE Spring is past, Dear Friend.   Eight hundred miles
  Divide us : we can watch no more together
The crimson lips **of** mountains drink the sun
Over the tideless **sea : no more can** mark

The glittering scales of moonlight on the breast
Of the green ocean, like the argent-clad
Breast of the Angel Michael—nor can hear,
(Pacing the beach, what time the small town slept)
The petulant sobbing of the little waves
That had not strength to reach the stones they know.

H. AÏDÉ.

[*From* By the Sea.]

THE sea, yon distant bar along,
　　Is moaning, like a heart in pain;
But rising, as a giant strong,
Soon shall the burthen of his song
　　Break on the shore again.

"Oblivion" is that burthen grand,
　　For ages, Love, unchanging still;
While reaching out a wrinkled hand,
He clean effaces from the sand
　　Our names,—as Time soon will!

H. AÏDÉ.

[*From* Seadrift.]

THE sea it moans over dead men's bones,
　　The sea it foams in anger;
The curlews swoop through the resonant air
　　With a warning cry of danger.

The starfish clings to the sea-weed's rings
  In a vague, dumb sense of peril;
And the spray, with its phantom-fingers, grasps
  At the mullein dry and sterile.

THOMAS BAILY ALDRICH.

[*From* The Voice of the Sea.]

IN the hush of the autumn night
    I hear the voice of the sea,
In the hush of the autumn night
It seems to say to me—
Mine are the winds above,
Mine are the caves below,
Mine are the dead of yesterday
And the dead of long ago!

T. B. ALDRICH.

[*From* The Wreck of the " Northern Belle."]

FAIR sight! from the rails,
    —When the Topman hails
" Land ho! on the larboard !"—to see
  The green waves leap
  At the white cliff's steep
On the shore of the land of the free :—
Fair music they make together,
  The cliff and the climbing foam ;

And it sounds in the bright blue weather
 Like the wanderer's welcome home.

But when the east wind howleth,
And the great seas rise and rave,
 Another sight
 Is that belt of white,
And another sound's on the wave;
 Small welcome for wildered vessel,
When the billows, giant and grey,
 Break—sworn on the sand
 Her keel to strand,
And her ribs on the rocks to lay !

Edwin Arnold.

[*From* The Twelve Months—May.]

WHO cares on the land to stay,
 Wasting the wealth of a day?
 The yellow fields leave
 For the meadows that heave,
And away to the sea—away !

To the meadows far out on the deep,
Whose ploughs are the winds that sweep
 The green furrows high,
 When into the sky
The silvery foam-bells leap.

At sea !—my bark—at sea !
With the winds, and the wild clouds and **me** ;
   The low shore soon
   Will be down with the moon,
And none on the waves but **we** ! . . .

On ! **on** ! with a swoop **and a swirl,**
High over the clear waves' curl ;
   Under thy prow,
   Like a fairy, now,
Make the blue water bubble with pearl !

E. ARNOLD.

[*From* The Forsaken Merman.]

COME, dear children, **let us away** ;
   Down and away below !
Now my brothers **call from the** bay,
Now the great winds shoreward blow,
Now the salt tides seaward flow ;
Now the wild white horses play,
Champ and chafe and toss in **the spray.**
Children dear, let us away !
This way, this way ! . . .
  .   .   .   .

Come away, away children ;
Come children, come down !
The hoarse wind blows coldly ;
Lights shine in the town.
She will start from her slumber

When gusts shake the door;
She will hear the winds howling,
Will hear the waves roar.
We shall see, while above us
The waves roar and whirl,
A ceiling of amber,
A pavement of pearl.
Singing : "Here came a mortal,
But faithless was she !
And alone dwell for ever
The kings of the sea."

But children, at midnight,
When soft the winds blow,
When clear falls the moonlight,
When spring-tides are low;
When sweet airs come seaward
From heaths starr'd with broom,
And high rocks throw mildly
On the blanch'd sands a gloom;
Up the still, glistening beaches,
Up the creeks we will hie,
Over banks of bright seaweed
The ebb-tide leaves dry.
We will gaze, from the sand-hills,
At the white, sleeping town;
At the church on the hill-side—
And then come back down.
Singing : " There dwells a loved one,
But cruel is she !

> She left lonely for ever
> The kings of the sea."
>
> MATTHEW ARNOLD.

[*From* Dover Beach.]

THE sea is calm to-night.
    The tide is full, the moon lies fair
Upon the straits ;—on the French coast the light
Gleams and is gone ; the cliffs of England stand,
Glimmering and vast, out in the tranquil bay.
Come to the window, sweet is the night-air !
Only, from the long line of spray
Where the sea meets the moon-blanch'd land,
Listen ! you hear the grating roar
Of pebbles which the waves draw back, and fling,
At their return, up the high strand,
Begin, and cease, and then again begin,
With tremulous cadence slow, and bring
The eternal note of sadness in.

Sophocles long ago
Heard it on the Ægæan, and it brought
Into his mind the turbid ebb and flow
Of human misery; we
Find also in the sound a thought,
Hearing it by this distant northern sea.
The Sea of Faith
Was once, too, at the full, and round earth's shore
Lay like the folds of a bright girdle furl'd.

But now I only hear
Its melancholy, long, withdrawing roar,
Retreating, to the breath
Of the night-wind, down the vast edges drear
And naked shingles of the world.

M. ARNOLD.

[*From* A Southern Night.]

THE sandy spits, the shore-lock'd lakes,
    Melt into open, moonlit sea ;
The soft Mediterranean breaks
  At my feet, free.

M. ARNOLD.

[*From* The Future.]

THE stars come out, and the night-wind
    Brings up the stream
Murmurs and scents of the infinite sea.

M. ARNOLD.

[*From* The New Sirens.]

THE howling levels
   Of the deep.

M. ARNOLD.

[*From* **Switzerland—**To Marguerite.]

THE unplumb'd, salt, estranging sea.

M. ARNOLD.

[*From* **The Human Tragedy, Act ii.**]

BUT when a sunny sevennight had passed,
    Up from the south there came a trailing **cloud,**
And in its train an ever-rising blast,
That soon was singing high in sail and shroud
And as it waxed, the sky grew overcast,
Lurid and low ;—whereat the breakers proud
Curved their strong crests, flung up their forelocks hoar,
And, madly rearing, plunged towards the shore.

And still as waned the day the wrathful ocean
Higher and higher rose, and to and fro
The slippery billows slid in shapeless motion,
Now dense and dark, now shivered into snow ;
Then once again as thick as hell-hag's potion,
Clotted with briny litter from below :
Like leaden coffins yawning first to sight,
Then swiftly hidden with fringed shrouds of white.

And where the sun would have been seen to set,
If sun had been, the sky was darkened most,
And drooped the welkin lower and lower yet,
As night stole on without her starry host.

Anon, with flapping wings and stormy threat,
Foul seagulls came, and screamed along the coast ;
Then utter dark closed in, before, behind,
And over all loud growled the wolfish wind.

'Twas midnight, and the waves were rolling in ;
But in the little town were none who slept,
Save dotage deaf or childhood free from sin.
Pale in their beds, the rest scared vigil kept,
Crossing themselves, and listening to the din ;
And, as it swelled, the women wailed and wept,
And wrung their hands, thinking of those at sea,
Then hushed their babes, waked by the threnody.

ALFRED AUSTIN.

[*From* The Human Tragedy, Act ii.]

FAR off, the silent sea gloomed cold and gray,
    Sky-sundered by one long low line of white.

A. AUSTIN.

[*From* The Human Tragedy, Act iii.]

THE tide comes rolling in, in ridgy sheets,
    Surge after surge, with hollow-bosomed roar,
Plunges and breaks, then hurriedly retreats,
And the stunned strand stands solid as before.

But swift a fresh on-coming billow meets
The flying foam, and carries it along,
Back to the assault, with volume doubly **strong.**

A. AUSTIN.

[*From* The Human Tragedy, Act iv.]

AND soon they were afresh upon the sea,
    Hearing no more discordant tongues of men,
But only ocean's plastic melody,
With wave attuned to **wave, attuned again**
To wave, where every **wave withal was free.**

A. AUSTIN.

[*From* Festus, ix.]

FESTUS. Away, away **upon the whitening tide,**
    Like lover hastening to **embrace his bride,**
We hurry faster than the foam we **ride;**
Dashing aside the waves which **round us cling,**
With strength like that which lifts an eagle's wing
Where the stars dazzle and the angels **sing.**
  Lucifer. We scatter the spray,
And break through the billows,
As the wind makes way
Through the leaves of willows.
  Festus. **In vain** they urge their armies to the fight;
Their surge-crests crumble 'neath our stroke of might.

G

We meet, fear not, we mount; now rise, now fall;
And dare with full-nerved arm the rage of all.
Through anger-swollen wave, or sparkling spray,
Nothing it recks; we hold our perilous way
Right onward till we feel the whirling brain
Ring with the maddening music of the main;
Till the fixed eyeball strives and strains to ken,
Yet loathes to see the shore and haunts of men;
And the blood, half starting through each ridgy vein
In the unwieldy hand, sets, black with pain.
Then let the tempest cloud on cloud come spread,
And tear the stormy terrors of his head;
Let the wild sea-bird wheel around my brow,
And shriek, and swoop, and flap her wing as now;
It gladdens.   On, ye boisterous billows, roll;
And keep my body, ye have ta'en my soul.
Thou element, the type which God hath given,
For eyes and hearts too earthy, of His heaven;
Were Heavén a mockery, never I would mourn
While o'er thy billows I might still be borne;
While yet to me the power and joy were given
To fling my breast on thine, and mingle earth with
    Heaven. . . .
The sea again, the swift bright sea! . . .
Look, listen! there is music in the cave,
Where ocean sleeps, and brightness in the wave,
The sea-bird makes its pillow, and the star,
Last born of Heaven, its azure mirror;—far
And wide, the pale, fine gleam of sea-fire glows,
Softly sublime, like lightnings in repose—

Till roused anon, afar its flaming spray **it throws.** . . .
 Lucifer. Well, now we have travelled above the waves,
Wilt travel a time beneath?
And visit the sea-born in their caves;
And look on the rainbow-tinted wreath
Of weed, pearl-starred, and gemmed wherewith
The mermaid binds her long green **hair?**
Or rouse the sea-snake from his lair?
See where he gambols for us **there!**
 Festus. Ay, ay; down let **us dive.** . . .
 Lucifer. Come on! **come on!** The dew last night
Was heavy.
 Festus.   **Are those spars so bright,**
Or eyes of things which ne'er forgive,
That seem to play on us, and glare
With rage, that we so far should **dare**
To search the hidden **deeps,**
Where tide, **the moon-slave, sleeps;**
And ork and **kraken,** world-forgotten, **live?**
Where the wind breathes not, **and the wave**
Walks softly, as above a grave;
Where coral worms, **in** countless nations,
Build rocks up from the sea's foundations;
Where the islands strike their roots
Far from the old mainland;
And spring **like** desert fruits,
Shook off by God's strong hand,
Up from their bed of sand.

PHILIP JAMES BAILEY.

A Song of the Sea.

" SAILOR, sailor, tell to me
　　　What sights have you seen on the mighty sea!"
" When the seas were calm and the skies were clear,
And the watch I've kept until day was near,
Eyes I have seen, black as yours, dear, are,
And a face I've looked on that was, how far !
　　That was, girl, oh ! how far from me !"

　　" Sailor, sailor, tell to me
　　What else have you seen on the far, far sea?"
" I've seen the flying-fish skim the brine,
And the great whales blow, and these eyes of mine
Have seen on the icebergs the north-lights play—
But often I've seen a home far away,
　　And a girl, oh, how dear to me !"

　　"Sailor, sailor, tell to me
　　The sounds men hear on the stormy sea."
" I've heard, my girl, the wild winds blow,
And the good ship creak to her keel below ;
But a laugh, too, I've heard, that, O well, well I know !
And a far, far voice—a voice that was, O
　　How sweet ! O how sweet to me !"

　　" Nay, tell me, sailor, tell to me
　　The sights and scenes of the wild, wild sea."
" Alike in calm, and breeze, and storm,

I've dream'd one dream and I've seen **one form**;
One dream that, dearest, shall soon be true,
One form that, my girl, I clasp in you,
That my own sweet wife shall be."

WILLIAM COX BENNETT.

[*From* Red-Cotton Night-Cap Country, Part i.]

WE stand upon an eminence,—
To where the earth-shell scallops out **the sea,**
A sweep of semicircle ; and **at edge—**
Just as the milk-white incrustations stud
At intervals some shell-extremity,
So do the little growths attract us here,
Towns with each name I told you : say, they touch
The sea, and the **sea them, and all is said,**
So sleeps and sets to slumber that broad **blue !**

ROBERT BROWNING.

[*From* Paracelsus, **Part v.**]

THE wroth sea's waves are edged
With foam, white as the bitten lip of Hate,
When in the solitary waste strange groups
Of young volcanos come up, cyclops-like,
Staring together with their eyes on flame.

R. BROWNING.

[*From* Pauline.]

L IKE a sea's arm as it goes rolling on,
    Being the pulse of some great country.
R. BROWNING.

[*From* Meeting at Night.]

T HE grey sea and the long black land;
    And the yellow half-moon large and low;
And the startled little waves that leap
In fiery ringlets from their sleep.
R. BROWNING.

[*From* In the Doorway.]

T HE water's in stripes like a snake, olive-pale
    To the leeward,—
On the weather-side, black, spotted white with the wind.
R. BROWNING.

[*From* Balder the Beautiful.]

Full Godhead.

H E crieth, " Far away methinks I mark
    A mighty forest dark,
Crown'd by a crimson mist; yonder it lies,
    Stretching into the skies,

And farther than its darkness nought I see."
    And softly answereth she,
" O Balder! 'tis the Ocean.   Vast and strange,
    It changeth without change,
Washing with weary waves for evermore
    The dark Earth's silent shore."

ROBERT BUCHANAN.

[*From* Balder the Beautiful.]

The Man by the Ocean.

CALMLY it lieth, limitless and deep,
    In windless summer sleep,
And from its fringe, cream-white and set with shells,
    A drowsy murmur swells,
While in its shallows, on its yellow sands,
    Smiling, uplifting hands,
Moves Balder, beckoning with bright looks and words
    The snow-white ocean-birds.
He smiles—the heavens smile answer !   All the sea
    Is glistering glassily.
Far out, blue-black amid the waters dim,
    Leviathan doth swim,
Spouts fountain-wise, roars loud, then sinking slow,
    Seeks the green depths below.

R. BUCHANAN.

[*From* The City Asleep.]

THROUGH all the thrilling waters creep
    Deep throbs of strange unrest,
Like washings of the windless Deep
    When it is peacefullest.

A little while—God's breath will go,
    And hush the flood no more ;
The dawn will break—the wind will blow,
    The Ocean rise and roar.

Each day with sounds of strife and death
    The waters rise and call ;
Each midnight, conquer'd by God's breath,
    To this dead calm they fall.

R. Buchanan.

For Music.

ALONG the shore, along the shore
    I see the wavelets meeting ;
But thee I see—ah, never more,
    For all my wild heart's beating.
The little wavelets come and go,
The tide of life ebbs to and fro,
    Advancing and retreating :

But from the shore, the steadfast shore,
   The sea is parted never :
And mine I hold thee evermore,
   For ever and for ever.

Along the shore, along the shore,
   I hear the waves resounding,
But thou wilt cross them never more
   For all my wild heart's bounding :
The moon comes out above the tide,
And quiets all the waters wide,
   Her pathway bright surrounding :
While on the shore, the dreary shore ;
   I walk with weak endeavour,
I have thy love's light evermore,
   For ever and for ever.

DINAH MARIA CRAIK.

Ocean.

MORE than bare mountains 'neath a naked sky,
   Or star-enchanted hollows of the night
When clouds are riven, or the most sacred light
Of summer dawns, art thou a mystery
And awe and terror and delight, O sea !
Our Earth is simple-hearted, sad to-day
Beneath the hush of snow, next morning gay
Because west-winds have promised to the lea

Violets and cuckoo-buds ; and sweetly these
Live innocent lives, each flower in its green field,
Joying as children in sun, air, and sleep.
But thou art terrible, with the unrevealed
Burden of dim lamentful prophecies,
And thy lone life is passionate and deep.

EDWARD DOWDEN.

[*From* The Castle.]

THE tenderest ripple touched and touched the shore ;
    The tenderest light was in the western sky ;—
Its one soft phrase, closing reluctantly,
The sea articulated o'er and o'er
To comfort all tired things ; and one might pore,
Till mere oblivion took the heart and eye,
On that slow-fading, amber radiancy
Past the long levels of the ocean floor.

E. DOWDEN.

[*From* The Heroines—Andromeda.]

THE wide
    Intolerable splendour of the sea,
Calm in a liquid hush of summer morn.

E. DOWDEN.

[*From* The Heroines—Europa.]

O SPLENDOUR of the multitudinous sea!

E. DOWDEN.

[*From* By the Sea—Evening.]

H USH! while the vaulted hollow of the **night**
  Deepens, what voice is this the sea sends **forth,**
Disconsolate iterance, a passionless moan?
Ah! now the Day is gone, and tyrannous **Light,**
  And the calm presence of fruit-bearing Earth:
  Cry, Sea! it is thy hour: thou art alone.

E. DOWDEN.

[*From* At Sea.]

O LD Ocean rolls like time, each billow passing
  Into another melts, and **is no more,**
Whilst the indwelling spirit works on, massing
  The great whole as before.

The separate waves are swift to come and go,
But the deep smiles, as they die one by one,
In lazy pleasure lifting from below
  His foam-flecked purple to the sun.

Eve comes, **the floods race** past, we see their white
Thrilled through by weird sea-fires, a burning shiver
Which **for** one moment **lives** in eager light
And then—is quenched for ever.
SIR FRANCIS HASTINGS DOYLE.

[*From* To a Sea-Bird.]

SAUNTERING hither on listless wings,
  Careless vagabond of the sea,
Little thou heed'st the surf that sings,
The bar that thunders, the shale that rings,—
  Give me to keep thy company. . . .

Lazily rocking on ocean's breast,
  Something in common, old friend, have we;
Thou on the shingle seek'st thy nest,
I to the waters look for rest,—
  I on the shore, and thou on the sea.
BRET HARTE.

[*From* Under the Waves.]

THROUGH wilds of silent sea-grass, rock, and sand,
  Where monsters swim and crawl—through slimy
    caves—
O'er peaks that cannot hear the sound of waves—
Low trails the Electric Wire from strand to strand,

Or festoons chasms wide-yawning **and** profound.
Darkling it trails 'mong shells and floating forms—
Over the dismal faces of the drown'd—
Cold fathoms down below the **reach of storms,**
Or tides deep-heaving at the moon's **command.**

And on the **mystic** path **of that fine line**
Go wondrous messages. **Far nations talk,**
As near as arm-link'd lovers in their walk,
Through twice a thousand miles of awful brine !
Man's speech through ocean flits, like light express'd
Through the rent cloud. Knit be the hearts as **now**
The exulting shores of England and the **West !**
Proud Science wears a glory **on her brow,**
As newly gifted with a power divine.

James Hedderwick.

[*From* The **Villa by the Sea.**]

FORWARD **how** the storm-god **urges**
  These his white steeds of the sea !

J. Hedderwick.

A Wave.

O BEING in thy dissolution known
    Most lovely then ;
O Life that ever has **to die alone,**
    To live again ;

O bounding Heart that still must bow and break
 To touch thine end;
O broken Purpose that must failure take,
 And deathward bend,
For the great tide to stretch from rock to rock
 His shining way;
O wandering Will that from the furthest shock
 Of sea-deeps grey,
Silver constraint of secret light on high
 Leads safe to shore;
O living Rapture that dost inly sigh,
 And evermore
Within thy joy the wailful voices keep;
 I see thee now,
O Son of the unfathomable deep!
 And trembling know
The crownèd Shadow of man's opposites,
 The forces dread
That sway him into being, blanched with lights
 Of thunder bred;
A poisèd Passion wrought from central breath
 Of whirling storms,
And evermore a deathless life in death,
 That still re-forms.
And thou, man's prototype in varying moods,
 Didst lonely beat
The vacant shores and speechless solitudes
 With silver feet,
Through the great æons wandering forlorn
 In search of him,

As rose and fell like vacant flames, lone morn
    An evening dim,
Ere light had grown articulate in love,
    Or silence knew
Herself as worship.   Then didst thou ever move
    Beneath the blue,
An incommunicable mystery,
    About thy shore;
A visible yearning of the earth and sea,
    That evermore
Flung out white arms to catch at some far good
    Yet unfulfilled,
And failing sobbed and sank in solitude
    With heart unstilled;
A voice that ever crying as of old
    In deserts dumb,
With hollow tongue reverberate foretold
    A Life to come.

ELLICE HOPKINS.

[*From* The High Tide.]

L**O** ! along the river's bed
    A mighty eygre reared his crest,
And uppe the Lindis raging sped.
It swept with thunderous noises loud;
Shaped like a curling snow-white cloud,
Or like a demon in a shroud.

And rearing Lindis backward pressed
  Shook all her trembling bankes amaine ;
Then madly at the eygre's breast
  Flung uppe **her** weltering walls again.
Then bankes **came** downe with ruin and **rout**—
Then beaten foam flew round **about**—
Then all the mighty floods were **out.**

So farre, so fast the eygre drave,
  The heart had hardly time to beat,
Before a shallow seething wave
  Sobbed in the grasses at oure feet :
The feet had hardly time to flee
Before it brake against the knee,
And all the world was in the sea.

JEAN INGELOW.

[*From* Gladys and Her Island.]

THE sea
  Was filled with light; in clear blue caverns curled
The breakers, and they ran, and seemed to romp,
As playing at some rough and dangerous game,
While all the nearer waves rushed in to help,
And all the farther heaved their heads to peep,
And tossed the fishing boats.

JEAN INGELOW.

[*From* Honours, Part i.]

THEN saunter down that terrace whence the sea
    All fair with wing-like sails you may discern ;
Be glad, and say, " This beauty is for me—
    A thing to love and learn.

" For me the bounding in of tides ; for me
    The laying bare of sands when they retreat ;
The purple flush of calms, the sparkling glee
    When waves and sunshine meet. "

JEAN INGELOW.

[*From* The Four Bridges.]

" OR I would sail upon the tropic seas,
    Where fathom long the blood-red dulses grow,
Droop from the rock and waver in the breeze,
    Lashing the tide to foam ; while calm below
The muddy mandrakes throng those waters warm,
And purple, gold, and green, the living blossoms swarm."

JEAN INGELOW.

From A Story of Doom, Book i.]

ROLLING among the furrows of the unquiet,
    Unconsecrate, unfriendly, dreadful sea.

JEAN INGELOW.

H

[*From* **The Dreams that Came True.**]

THE long
    Illimitable reaches of " the vasty deep."
JEAN INGELOW.

[*From* **Love the Vampire.**]

THE level sands and grey,
    Stretch leagues and leagues away,
Down to the border line of sky and foam,
    A spark of sunset burns,
    The grey tide-water turns,
Back, like a ghost from her forbidden home !
ANDREW LANG.

[*From* **The Sirens.**]

THE sea is lonely, the sea is dreary,
    The sea is restless and uneasy ;
Thou seekest quiet, thou art weary,
Wandering thou knowest not whither ;—
Our little isle is green and breezy,
Come and rest thee ! O come hither,
Come to this peaceful home of ours,
    Where evermore
The low west-wind creeps panting up the shore

To be at rest among the flowers.

  .   .   .   .

Look how the grey **old Ocean**
From the depth of his heart rejoices,
Heaving with a gentle motion,
When he hears our restful voices;
List how he sings in an undertone,
Chiming with our melody;
And all sweet sounds of earth and **air**
Melt into one low voice alone,
That murmurs over the weary sea,
And seems to sing from everywhere—
" Here mayst thou harbour peacefully,
Here mayst thou rest from the aching oar ;
    Turn thy curvëd prow ashore,
And in our **green isle rest for evermore !**
      For evermore !"
And Echo half wakes in the wooded hill,
    And, to her heart so calm and deep,
    Murmurs over **in her sleep,**
Doubtfully pausing and **murmuring still,**
     " Evermore !**"**
    Thus, on Life's weary **sea,**
    Heareth the marinere
    Voices sweet, from far and near,
    Ever singing low and clear,
    Ever singing longingly.

Is it not better here to be,
Than to be toiling late and soon ?

In the dreary night to see
Nothing but the blood-red moon
Go up and down into the sea ;
Or, in the loneliness of the day,
 To see the still seals only
Solemnly lift their faces grey,
 Making it yet more lonely ?
Is it not better than to hear
Only the sliding of the wave
Beneath the plank, and feel so near
A cold and lonely grave,
A restless grave, where thou shalt lie
Even in death unquietly ?
Look down beneath thy wave-worn bark,
 Lean over the side and see
The leaden eye of the sidelong shark
 Upturnëd patiently,
Ever waiting there for thee :
Look down and see those shapeless forms,
 Which ever keep their dreamless sleep
 Far down amid the gloomy deep,
And only stir themselves in storms,
Rising like islands from beneath,
And snorting through the angry spray,
As the frail vessel perisheth
In the whirls of their unwieldy play ;
  Look down ! look down !
Upon the sea-weed, slimy and dark,
That waves its arms so lank and brown,
 Beckoning for thee !

Look down beneath thy wave-worn bark
Into the cold depths of the sea !
Look down ! look down !
Thus, on life's lonely sea,
Heareth the marinere
Voices sad, from far and near,
Ever singing full of fear,
Ever singing drearfully.

James Russell Lowell.

[*From* The Shore.]

THE roar of the limitless sea.

Robert, Earl of Lytton.

[*From* Sea-Side Elegiacs.]

WHEN, at the mid o' the night, high on the shadowy land,
Mournfully watching the ghost-like waves. livid-lipp'd, hollow-breasted,
Sob over shingle and shell, here with my sorrow I stand.
Weary of woe that is in them, fatigued by the violent weathers,
Feebly they tumble and toss, sadly they murmur and moan.

Earl of Lytton.

[*From* A Night in a Fisherman's Hut.]

HARK ! the horses of ocean that crouch at my feet,
  They are moaning in impotent pain on the beach !

EARL OF LYTTON.

[*From* The Journey.]

JOY ! O joy ! the dawning sea
    Answers to the dawning sky ;
Foretaste of the coming glee
When the sun will lord it high.
See the swelling radiance grow
To a dazzling glory-might !
Thoughtful shadows gently go
'Twixt the wave-tops wild with light !

Hear the strutting billows clang !
See the falling billows lean
Half a watery vault, and hang
Gleaming with translucent green—
Then in thousand fleeces lie,
Thundering light upon the strand !—
Vague it reached my doubting eye
Through the dusk, across the land.

GEORGE MACDONALD.

[*From* England and Louis Napoleon.]

HOW proud in peace,
    The wild white horses rear and foam along.
                      GERALD MASSEY.

[*From* A Day at Craigcrook Castle.]

THE silvery-green and violet-sheen o' the sea
    Changed into shifting opal tinct with gold ;
And like an Alchymist with furnace-face
The sun smiled on his perfect work, pure gold.
                      GERALD MASSEY.

[*From* Nelson.]

LIKE one vast sapphire flashing light,
    The sea, just breathing, shone.
                      GERALD MASSEY.

[*From* Modern Love.]

YONDER midnight ocean's force,
    Thundering like ramping hosts of warrior horse,
To throw that faint thin line upon the shore.
                    GEORGE MEREDITH.

[*From* Sea Voices.]

PEACE, moaning Sea ; what tale have you to tell?
　　What mystic tidings, all unknown before?
　Whether you break in thunder on the shore,
Or whisper like the voice within the shell,
O moaning Sea, I know your burden well.

'Tis but the old dull tale, filled full of pain ;
　The finger on the dial-plate of time,
　Advancing slow with pitiless beat sublime,
As stoops the day upon the fading plain ;
And that has been which may not be again.

LEWIS MORRIS.

[*From* The Life and Death of Jason, Book iv.]

O BITTER sea, tumultuous sea,
　　Full many an ill is wrought by thee !—
　Unto the wasters of the land
　Thou holdest out thy wrinkled hand ;
　And when they leave the conquered town,
　Whose black smoke makes thy surges brown,
　Driven betwixt thee and the sun,
　As the long day of blood is done,
　From many a league of glittering waves
　Thou smilest on them and their slaves.
　" The thin bright-eyed Phœnician

Thou drawest to thy waters wan,
With ruddy eve and golden morn
Thou temptest him, until, forlorn,
Unburied, under alien skies
Cast up ashore his body lies.
Yea, **whoso** seeks thee from his door,
Must ever long for more and more ;
Nor will the beechen bowl suffice,
Or homespun robe of **little price,**
Or hood well-woven of the fleece
Undyed, or unspiced wine of Greece ;
So sore his heart is set upon
Purple, and gold, and cinnamon ;
For as thou cravest, so he craves,
Until he **rolls** beneath thy waves.
Nor in some landlocked, unknown bay,
Can satiate thee **for one day.**

" Now, therefore, O thou bitter sea,
With no long words we pray to thee,
But ask thee, hast thou **felt** before
Such strokes of the long ashen oar ?
And hast thou yet seen such a prow
Thy rich and niggard waters plough ?
" Nor yet, O sea, shalt thou be **cursed,**
If at thy hands we gain the worst,
And, wrapt in water, roll about
Blind-eyed, unheeding song or shout,
Within thine eddies far from shore,
Warmed by no sunlight any more.

" Therefore, indeed, we **joy** in thee,
And **praise** thy greatness, and will we
Take at thy hands both good and ill,
Yea, what thou wilt, and praise **thee still,**
Enduring not to sit **at home,**
And wait until **the last days come,**
When we no more may care **to hold**
White bosoms under **crowns of gold,**
And **our** dulled hearts **no longer are**
Stirred by the clangorous noise of war,
And hope within our souls is dead,
And no joy is rememberèd.

" So, if thou hast a mind to slay,
Fair prize thou hast of us to-day;
And if thou hast a mind to save,
Great praise and honour shalt thou have;
But whatso thou wilt do with us,
Our end shall not be piteous,
Because our memories shall live
When folk forget the way to drive
The black keel through the heaped-up sea,
And half dried up thy waters be."

WILLIAM MORRIS.

[*From* The Life and Death of Jason,
Book xiv.]

THE tyrannous and conquered sea.

W. MORRIS.

[*From* The Life and Death of Jason, Book xiv.]

The Sirens.

IF ye be bold with us to go,
   Things such as happy dreams may show
Shall your once heavy eyes behold
About our palaces of gold ;
Where waters 'neath the waters run,
And from o'erhead a harmless sun
Gleams through the woods of chrysolite.
There gardens fairer to the sight
Than those of the Phæacian king
Shall ye behold ; and, wondering,
Gaze on the sea-born fruit and flowers,
And thornless and unchanging bowers,
Whereof the Maytime knoweth nought,
   So to the pillared house being brought,
Poor souls, ye shall not be alone,
For o'er the floors of pale blue stone
All day such feet as ours shall pass,
And, 'twixt the glimmering walls of glass,
Such bodies garlanded with gold,
So faint, so fair, shall ye behold,
And clean forget the treachery
Of changing earth and tumbling sea.

W. MORRIS.

Alone by the Bay.

HE is gone.   O my heart, he is gone ;
    And the sea remains and the sky,
And the skiffs flit in and out,
    And the white-winged yachts go by.

The waves run purple and green,
    And the sunshine glints and glows,
And freshly across the bay
    The breath of the morning blows.

I liked it better last night,
    When the dark shut down on the main,
And the phantom fleet lay still,
    And I heard the waves complain.

For the sadness that dwells in my heart,
    And the rune of their endless woe,—
Their longing and void and despair,—
    Kept time in their ebb and flow.
                 LOUISE CHANDLER MOULTON.

[*From* Etretat.]

THE ocean beats against the stern, dumb shore,
    The stormy passion of its mighty heart.
                 L. C. MOULTON.

High Tide at Midnight.

NO breath is on the glimmering ocean-floor,
  No blast beneath the windless Pleiades,
But thro' dead night a melancholy roar,
  A voice of moving and of marching seas,—
The boom of thundering waters on the shore,
  Sworn with slow force by desolate degrees
Once to go on, and whelm for evermore
  Earth and her folk and all their phantasies.
Then half asleep in the great sound I seem
Lost in the starlight, dying in a dream
  Where overmastering powers abolish me,—
Drown, and thro' dim euthanasy redeem
My merged life in the living ocean-stream,
  And soul environing of shadowy sea.

FREDERICK W. H. MYERS.

[*From* A Sea Symphony—Tempest.]

GRAND lion-leap of billows ! how they fall,
  Plunging with hunger to devour the shore !
Hurled mountain of blown billow thwart the wall
Of cliff precipitous bursting with stupendous roar !
Cavernous halls of hoary mountains under
Shake with a shock of subterraneous thunder,
Rumble with roll of long reverberate thunder !
Crushed all the turbid water-mountain toils,
Whose slain, immense, pale, shadowy ghost is thrown

High among hurrying storm-cloud, and recoils
Seethingly, limply plashing on the stone.
While underneath a baffled field of foam,
Poured out disorderly, retreats to rise
One fulvous mass of spume upon a dome
Of wave colossal threatening the skies :
Lo ! as it sweeps imperial, the curl
In toppling hangs arrested by a swirl,
Refluent baffled ; rears aloft to hurl
All, one grim rampart perpendicular,
Bodily heavenward, whose wrestling froth,
In terrible welter of tumultuous wrath,
Flickers to momentary crags of spar,
Headlong to ruin charges with an ocean jar,
A headlong ruin of water, heard inland afar !

Hon. Roden Noel.

[*From* A Sea Symphony—Twilight.]

INFINITE, pale, and dim and desolate,
   Monotonous Ocean, with the Voice of Fate,
Breathes homeless, helpless, and disconsolate.

Hon. R. Noel.

[*From* The Children by the Sea.]

AH ! merry children on the smooth sea sand,
   Floating toy-navies, with your spades of wood
Delving until the salt sea-water stand
   In moat-like hollows, with a mimic flood

Girdling a mimic fort ; or gathering shells
   And briny delicate sea-weed ; how the air
Blows in glad faces, and the wave compels
   Your flight with laughter, leaving a crystal rare
   Upon the ripple-pencilled sand ! how fair
Life **seems, the** very weary life we know,
   In your exuberant play, that loves to **feign**
Age has arrived !   Ah ! life **will never glow**
   For you **as** now when you are old ; remain
Children for ever ! **common** things **ye deem**
   Miraculous joy ; battle and storm **and death,**
With swift bright **gesture, eager eyes, ye dream !**
Breeze blows bright hair **of curled blue** billows **too ;**
But sparkling waves **less merrily dance than you !**
                  Hon. R. Noel.

[*From* At Lyme Regis.]

CALM, azure, marble sea,
   As a fair palace pavement largely **spread,**
Where the gray bastions of the eternal hills
   Lean over languidly,
Bosom'd with leafy trees, and garlanded !

   Peace **is** on all **I** view ;
Sunshine and peace ; earth clear as heaven one hour ;
Save where the sailing cloud its dusky line
   Ruffles along the blue,
Brush'd by the soft wing **of** the silent shower.

> In no profounder calm
> Did the great Spirit over ocean brood,
> Ere the first hill his yet unclouded crest
> Rear'd, or the first fair palm
> Doubled her maiden beauty in the flood.

FRANCIS TURNER PALGRAVE.

[*From* Wind and Wave.]

AND all the subtle zephyr hurries gay,
    And all the heaving ocean heaves one way,
T'ward the void sky-line and an unguess'd weal ;
Until the vanward billows feel
The agitating shallows, and divine the goal,
And to foam roll,
And spread and stray
And traverse wildly, like delighted hands,
The fair and fleckless sands ;
And so the whole
Unfathomable and immense
Triumphing tide comes at the last to reach
And burst in wind-kiss'd splendours on the deaf'ning beach,
Where forms of children in first innocence
Laugh and fling pebbles on the rainbow'd crest
Of its untired unrest.

COVENTRY PATMORE.

[*From* A Wedding Sermon.]

THE truths of Love are like the sea
For clearness and for mystery.

COVENTRY PATMORE.

The Sea's Bride.

ADA dreams by the sea-beach
(How far out the ripples reach !)
She is very sweet ;
Comes a wave with opal lips
Murmuring of shells and ships,
Kissing Ada's feet.

Ada sleeps by the sea-beach.
(How close up the ripples reach—
Will they never turn ?)
Phosphor lamps begin to shine,
Glance and flow the coraline,
Till the liquid lengths of brine
Into flashes burn.

Ada wakes by the sea-beach,
Round and round the deep waves reach,
Sways the eddying tide,
Clasps and clings the amber weed ;
Prays the maiden—she has need,
'Mid the waters wide.

I

Sea, thine arms are very soft ;
Wave, thy kisses wake not oft ;
Rock her, billow, soft and slow ;
Surge, sing to her light and low,
          Cheer thy bonny bride.
                    H. CHOLMONDELEY PENNELL.

[*From* Stornelli and Strambotti.]

" AS beats the sea against the rocks ! " you cried,
      " Against your stubborn will my soul is hurl'd."
You meant the seeming-daunted broken tide,
With scattered spray and shattered crests uncurl'd,
That, from the shore, we pity or deride ;
And yet these dying waters, spent and swirl'd,
Their stony limits do themselves decide,
And fashion to their will the unconscious world.
                    A. MARY F. ROBINSON.

[*From* Apprehension.]

EVEN such to thee am I ; but thou to me
      As the embracing shore to the sobbing sea,
Even as the sea itself to the stone-tossed rill.
But who, but who shall give such rest to thee ?
The deep mid-ocean waters perpetually
Call to the land, and call unanswered still.
                    A. M. F. ROBINSON.

[*From* The New Arcadia, Prologue.]

NOT where they clash ashore, and break and moan,
    Are waters deadliest.
A. M. F. ROBINSON.

[*From* Song.]

OH what comes over the sea,
    Shoals and quicksands past ;
And what comes home to me,
    Sailing slow, sailing fast?

A wind comes over the sea
    With a moan in its blast ;
But nothing comes home to me,
    Sailing slow, sailing fast.
CHRISTINA ROSSETTI.

[*From* By the Sea.]

WHY does the sea moan evermore?
    Shut out from heaven it makes its moan,
It frets against the boundary shore ;
    All earth's full rivers cannot fill
    The sea, that drinking thirsteth still.
CHRISTINA ROSSETTI.

A Storm at Sea.

GREAT clouds, like war-ships, speed athwart the sky,
   And the white drift, a full-set mainsail, gleams :
The savage blast, through the taut cordage screams,
Or fitful moans with melancholy cry :
Around, the raging waters foaming lie
In frenzied wrath, and not a sun-ray beams.
The mother, in her broken slumber, dreams
Of her dear sailor, shuddering lest he die !
Ocean runs riot ! and the bruiséd waves
Are blue and green with overmastering blows ;
The tangled weeds, disturbed, torn from their bed
A hundred fathoms down 'mid sailors' graves,
Toss here and there, as light as fresh-fallen snows,
And dismal caves disgorge their prisoned dead.

                          EARL OF ROSSLYN.

[*From* The Wreck.]

ITS masts of might, its sails so free,
   Had borne the scathless keel
Through many a day of darkened sea,
   And many a storm of steel ;
When all the winds were calm it met
   (With home returning prore)

With the lull
Of the waves
On a low lee shore.

.   .   .   .

The voices of the night are mute
  Beneath the moon's eclipse ;
The silence of the fitful flute
  Is on the dying lips.
The silence of my lonely heart
  Is kept for evermore
    In the lull
    Of the waves
  On a low lee shore.

JOHN RUSKIN.

[*From* Song.]

I LOVE the eddying circling sweep,
  The mantling and the foam
Of murmuring waters dark and deep
  Amid the valleys lone.

It is a terror, yet 'tis sweet
  Upon some broken brow
To look upon the distant sweep
  Of ocean spread below.

RUSKIN.

The Sea.

THESE froward waves, we feign they try
   To utter to us some mystery :
Such is the euphuistic game
We baffled poets follow :—
Pantheistic ! all the same,
Like the sounding cymbal hollow :—
We it is and not the sea
Long to speak out God's mystery :
Immense and world-old salt ocean,
With thy moon-adoring motion,
Thou hast nought to us to say,
We must speak and thou obey.

WILLIAM BELL SCOTT.

[*From* Better than Good.]

IT is better than good when the heart is drear
   To wander alone by the ocean's side ;
Where clamorous sea-mews sailing near
Make mournful music to meet the tide,
Which rolls to the rocks with a witless glide,
And roars, and batters the steadfast stone,
And broken falls as the boulders guide ;
While in creek and cavern the waters moan,
And the dungeoned tempests howl and groan.

EARL OF SOUTHESK.

[*From* Andromeda.]

THE wandering billows on the sea
   Ran laughingly and leapt.

EARL OF SOUTHESK.

[*From* Surf.]

SPLENDOURS of morning the billow-crests brighten,
   Lighting and luring them on to the land,—
Far-away waves where the wan vessels whiten,
   Blue rollers breaking in surf where **we stand**.
Curved like the necks of a legion of horses,
   Each with his froth-gilded mane flowing free,
Hither they speed in perpetual **courses**,
   Bearing thy riches, **O beautiful sea**!

Strong with the striving of yesterday's surges,
   Lashed by the wanton winds leagues from the shore,
Each, driven fast by its follower, urges
   Fearlessly those that are fleeting before;
How they leap over the ridges we walk on,
   Flinging us gifts from the depths of the sea,—
Silvery fish for the foam-hunting falcon,
   Palm-weed and pearls for my darling and me!

EDMUND CLARENCE STEDMAN.

[*From* The Mountain.]

THE great, encircling, radiant **sea**,
  Alone in its immensity.

E. C. STEDMAN.

[*From* On the Sea-Shore.]

UPON the rocky shore I sit alone ;
  The dark green sullen **sea**
Along the shore makes a perpetual **moan**
  And struggles restlessly. . . .

Across the purple shoals of sunken rocks
  The toppling racers break,
And suck, and **roar**, and beat **with** ceaseless shocks
  The worn cliff's weedy base.

Heaved by the lifting swell, the long green flag
  Of sea-weed floats **and falls,**
And down their shelf the **raking pebbles drag,**
  As back the surf-wave crawls.

Something there is beneath that constant moan
  That **utterance seeks in vain ;**
Like some **dim memory, some hidden tone**
  That, helpless, haunts the brain.

WILLIAM WETMORE STORY.

[*From* Off Shore.]

WHEN the might of the summer
    Is most on the sea;
When the days overcome her
    With joy but to be,
With rapture of royal enchantment, and sorcery that sets her
    not free,

    But for hours upon hours
      As a thrall she remains
    Spell-bound as with flowers
      And content in their chains,
And her loud steeds fret not, and lift not a lock of their
    deep white manes;

    Then only, far under
      In the depths of her hold,
    Some gleam of its wonder
      Man's eye may behold,
Its wild-weed forests of crimson and russet and olive and gold.

    Still deeper and dimmer
      And goodlier they glow,
    For the eyes of the swimmer
      Who scans them below
As he crosses the zone of their flowerage that knows not of
    sunshine and snow.

Soft blossomless frondage
   And foliage that gleams
As to prisoners in bondage
   The light of their dreams,
The desire of a dawn unbeholden, with hope on the wings
   of its beams.

Not as prisoners entombed,
   Waxen haggard and wizen,
But consoled and illumed
   In the depths of their prison
With delight of the light everlasting and vision of dawn on
   them risen,

From the banks and the beds
   Of the waters divine
They lift up their heads
   And the flowers of them shine
Through the splendour of darkness that clothes them, of
   water that glimmers like wine.

Bright bank over bank
   Making glorious the gloom,
Soft rank upon rank,
   Strange bloom after bloom,
They kindle the liquid low twilight, the dusk of the dim
   sea's womb.

Through the subtle and tangible
   Gloom without form,
Their branches, infrangible

Ever of storm,
Spread softer their sprays than the **shoots of the woodland
when** April is warm.

As the flight of the thunder, full
Charged with its **word,**
Dividing the wonderful
Depths like a bird,
Speaks wrath and delight to the heart of the night that **exults**
to have heard,

So swiftly, though soundless,
In silence's **car,**
Light, winged **from the boundless**
Blue depths full of cheer,
Speaks joy to the heart of the waters that part not **before**
him, **but hear.**

Light, perfect, **and visible**
Godhead **of God,**
God indivisible,
Lifts but his **rod,**
And the shadows are scattered in sunder, **and darkness is**
light at his nod.

ALGERNON CHARLES SWINBURNE.

[*From* The Triumph of Time.]

I WILL go back to the great sweet **mother,**
Mother and lover of men, the sea.
I will go down to her, I and none other,
Close to her, kiss her and mix her with me ;

Cling to her, strive with her, hold her fast;
O fair white mother, in days long past
Born without sister, born without brother,
　Set free my soul as thy soul is free.

O fair green-girdled mother of mine,
　Sea, that art clothed with the sun and the rain,
Thy sweet hard kisses are strong like wine,
　Thy large embraces are keen like pain.
Save me and hide me with all thy waves,
Find me one grave of thy thousand graves,
Those pure cold populous graves of thine,
　Wrought without hand in a world without stain.

I shall sleep, and move with the moving ships,
　Change as the winds change, veer in the tide;
My lips will feast on the foam of thy lips,
　I shall rise with thy rising, with thee subside;
Sleep, and not know if she be, if she were,
Filled full with life to the eyes and hair,
As a rose is fulfilled to the roseleaf tips,
　With splendid summer and perfume and pride.

This woven raiment of nights and days,
　Were it once cast off and unwound from me,
Naked and glad would I walk in thy ways,
　Alive and aware of thy ways and thee;
Clear of the whole world, hidden at home,
Clothed with the green and crowned with the foam,
A pulse of the life of thy straits and bays,
　A vein in the heart of the streams of the sea.

Fair mother, fed with the lives of men,
   Thou art subtle and cruel of heart, men say
Thou hast taken, and shalt not render again ;
   Thou art full of thy dead, and cold as they,
But death **is the** worst that comes of thee ;
Thou art fed with our dead, O mother, **O sea,**
But when hast thou fed on our hearts? **or when,**
   Having given us love, hast thou taken away?

O tender-hearted, **O perfect lover,**
   Thy lips are bitter, and sweet thine **heart.**
The hopes that hurt and the dreams that **hover,**
   Shall they not vanish away and apart?
But thou, thou art sure, thou art older than **earth ;**
Thou art **strong for death, and fruitful of birth ;**
Thy depths conceal and thy gulfs discover ;
   From **the first thou wert ; in the end thou art.**

SWINBURNE.

[*From* In the Water.]

THE sea is awake, and the sound of the **song** of the joy
   of her waking is rolled
From afar to the star that recedes, from anear to the wastes
   of the wild wide shore.
Her call is a trumpet compelling us homeward : if dawn in
   her east be acold,
From the sea shall we crave not her grace to rekindle **the**
   life that it kindled before,

Her breath to requicken, her bosom to rock us, her kisses to
  bless as of yore?
For the wind, with his wings half open, at pause in the sky,
  neither fettered nor free,
Leans waveward and flutters the ripple to laughter : and fain
  would the twain of us be
Where lightly the wave yearns forward from under the curve
  of the deep dawn's dome,
And, full of the morning and fired with the pride of the glory
  thereof and the glee,
Strike out from the shore as the heart in us bids and be-
  seeches, athirst for the foam.

Life holds not an hour that is better to live in : the past is
  a tale that is told,
The future a sun-flecked shadow, alive and asleep, with a
  blessing in store.
As we give us again to the waters, the rapture of limbs that
  the waters enfold
Is less than the rapture of spirit whereby, though the burden
  it quits were sore,
Our souls and the bodies they wield at their will are ab-
  sorbed in the life they adore—
In the life that endures no burden, and bows not the forehead, and bends not the knee—
In the life everlasting of earth and of heaven, in the laws
  that atone and agree,
In the measureless music of things, in the fervour of forces
  that rest or that roam,

That cross and return and reissue, as I after you and as you
    after me
Strike out from the shore as the heart in us bids and be-
    seeches, athirst for the foam. . . .
Friend, earth is a harbour of refuge for winter, a cover
    whereunder to flee
When day is the vassal of night, and the strength of the hosts
    of her mightier than he ;
But here is the presence adored of me, here my desire is at
    rest and at home.
There are cliffs to be climbed upon land, there are ways to
    be trodden and ridden : but we
Strike out from the shore as the heart in us bids and be-
    seeches, athirst for the foam.

SWINBURNE.

[*From* By the North Sea, Part i.]

I.

FOR the sea too seeks and rejoices,
    Gains and loses and gains,
And the joy of her heart's own choice is
    As ours, and as ours are her pains :
As the thoughts of our heart are her voices,
    And as hers is the pulse of our veins.

II.

Her fields that know not of dearth
    Nor lie for their fruit's sake fallow,
Laugh large in the depth of their mirth :

But inshore here in the shallow,
  Embroiled with encumbrance of earth,
    Their skirts are turbid and yellow.

III.

The grime of her greed is upon her,
  The sign of her deed is her soil;
As the earth's is her own dishonour,
  And corruption the crown of her toil:
She hath spoiled and devoured, and her honour
  Is this, to be shamed by her spoil.

IV.

But afar, where pollution is none,
  Nor sign of strife, nor endeavour,
Where her heart and the suns are one,
  And the soil of her sin comes never,
She is pure as the wind and the sun,
  And her sweetness endureth for ever.

SWINBURNE.

[*From* At a Month's End.]

WITH chafe and change of surges chiming,
  The clashing channels rocked and rang
Large music, wave to wild wave timing,
  And all the choral water sang.

Faint lights fell this way, that way floated,
  Quick sparks of sea-fire keen like eyes,

From the rolled surf that flashed, and noted
　　Shores and faint cliffs and bays and skies.

The ghost of sea that shrank up sighing,
　　At the sand's edge, a short sad breath
Trembling to touch the goal, and dying
　　With weak heart heaved up once in death.

SWINBURNE.

[*From* In Guernsey.]

M Y mother sea, my fostress, what new strand,
　　What new delight of waters, may this be,
The fairest found since time's first breezes fanned
　　My mother sea?

Once more I give me body and soul to thee,
Who hast my soul for ever: cliff and sand
Recede, and heart to heart once more are we.

My heart springs first and plunges, ere my hand
Strike out from shore: more close it brings to me,
More near and dear than seems my fatherland,
　　My mother sea.

SWINBURNE.

[*From* Anactoria.]

A ND shudder of water that makes felt on land
　　The immeasurable tremor of all the sea.

SWINBURNE.

K

[*From* Evenings on the Broad.]

INLAND glimmer the shallows asleep and afar in the
    breathless
  Twilight : yonder the depths darken afar and asleep.
Slowly the semblance of death out of heaven descends on
    the deathless
  Waters : hardly the light lives on the face of the deep.
SWINBURNE.

[*From* Tristram of Lyonesse.]

The Sailing of the Swallow.

AND the sea thrilled us with heart-sundering sighs,
    One after one drawn, with each breath it drew,
And the green hardened into iron blue,
And the soft light went out of all its face.
SWINBURNE.

[*From* Tristram of Lyonesse.]

The Queen's Pleasance.

AND all the sea lay subject to the sun.
SWINBURNE.

[*From* Philip Van Artevelde, Act 1, Sc. x.]

THE weltering of the restless wave.

SIR HENRY TAYLOR.

BREAK, break, break,
  On thy cold gray stones, **O Sea !**
And I would that my tongue could utter
  The thoughts that arise in me.

O well for the fisherman's boy,
  That **he shouts with his sister at play !**
O well for the sailor lad,
  That he sings in his boat on the bay !

And the stately ships go **on**
  To their haven under the hill ;
But O for the touch of a vanish'd hand,
  And the sound of a voice that is still !

Break, break, break,
  At the foot of thy crags, O Sea !
But the tender grace **of a** day that is dead
  Will never **come back to me.**

ALFRED, LORD TENNYSON.

[*From* A Dream of Fair Women.]

SO shape chased shape as swift as, when to land
    Bluster the winds and tides the self-same way,
Crisp foam-flakes scud along the level sand,
    Torn from the fringe of spray.

LORD TENNYSON.

[*From* The Palace of Art.]

ONE show'd an iron coast and angry waves.
    You seem'd to hear them climb and fall
And roar rock-thwarted under bellowing caves,
    Beneath the windy wall.

LORD TENNYSON.

[*From* The Merman.]

WHO would be
        A merman bold,
Sitting alone,
Singing alone,
Under the sea,
With a crown of gold,
On a throne?

I would be a merman bold,
I would sit and sing the whole of the day;
I would fill the sea-halls with a voice of power;
But at night I would roam abroad and play
With the mermaids **in and out** of the rocks,
Dressing their hair with the white sea flower;
And holding them back by their flowing locks
I would kiss them often under **the sea,**
And kiss them again till they kiss'd me
  Laughingly, laughingly;
And then we would wander away, away
To the pale green sea-groves straight and high,
  Chasing each other merrily.

LORD TENNYSON.

[*From* The Mermaid.]

WHO would be
    A mermaid **fair,**
Singing alone,
Combing her hair
Under the sea,
In a golden curl
With a comb of pearl,
On a throne?

I would **be** a mermaid fair;
I would sing to myself the whole of the day;
With a comb of pearl I would comb my hair;
And still as I comb'd I would **sing and** say,

"Who is it loves me? who loves not me?"
I would comb my hair till my ringlets would fall
  Low adown, low adown,
From under my starry sea-bud crown,
  Low adown and around,
And I should look like a fountain of gold,
      Springing alone
       With a shrill inner sound,
       Over the throne
       In the midst of the hall;
Till that great sea-snake under the sea
From his coiled sleeps in the central deeps
Would slowly trail himself seven-fold
Round the hall where I sate, and look in at the gate
With his large calm eyes for the love of me.
And all the mermen under the sea
Would feel their immortality
Die in their hearts for the love of me.

                    LORD TENNYSON.

[*From* The Voyage.]

FAR ran the naked moon across
  The houseless ocean's heaving field.

.   .   .   .   .   .

Across the boundless east we drove,
Where those long swells of breaker weep
  The nutmeg rocks and isles of clove.

.   .   .   .   .   .

By sands and streaming flats, and floods
Of mighty mouth, we scudded fast.

.   .   .   .   .

At times the whole sea burn'd, at times
With wakes of fire we tore the dark.

LORD TENNYSON.

[*From* The Passing **of Arthur.**]

ONLY the wan **wave**
Brake in . . . rolling far along the gloomy shores,
The voice **of days of** old and days to **be.**

LORD TENNYSON.

[*From* **The Passing of Arthur.**]

THE phantom circle of a moaning sea.

LORD TENNYSON.

[*From* The Last **Tournament.**]

O SWEETER than all memories of thee,
Deeper than any yearnings after thee,
Seem'd those far-rolling, westward-smiling seas.

LORD TENNYSON.

[*From* The Holy Grail.]

HEAPT in mounds and ridges all the sea
    Drove like a cataract.

LORD TENNYSON.

[*From* Lancelot and Elaine.]

BARE, as a wild wave in the wide North-sea,
    Green-glimmering toward the summit, bears, with all
Its stormy crests that smoke against the skies,
Down on a bark.

LORD TENNYSON.

[*From* Enoch Arden.]

THE low moan of leaden-colour'd seas.

LORD TENNYSON.

[*From* The Lover's Tale, Part i.]

THE incorporate blaze of sun and sea.

LORD TENNYSON.

[*From* In Memoriam, xxxv.]

THE moanings of the homeless sea.

LORD TENNYSON.

[*From* Maud, Part i.]

THE liquid azure bloom of a crescent of sea,
The silent sapphire-spangled marriage-ring of the land.

LORD TENNYSON.

[*From* Early **Spring.**]

THE deep,
All down the sand,
Is breathing in his sleep,
Heard by the land.

LORD TENNYSON.

Hymn to Ocean.

O CRADLE, whence the suns **ascend, old Ocean divine ;**
O grave, whereto the suns **descend, old Ocean divine :**

O spreading in the calm of night thy mirror, wherein
The Moon her countenance doth bend, old Ocean divine.

O thou that dost in midnights still thy chorus of waves
With dances of the planet blend, old **Ocean divine :**

The morning and the evening blooms are roses of thine,
Two roses that for thine are kenned, old Ocean divine.

O Aphrodite's panting breast, whose breathing doth make
The waves to fall and ascend, old Ocean divine.

O womb of Aphrodite, bear thy beautiful child,
Abroad thy glory to commend, old Ocean divine.

O sprinkle thou with pearly dew Earth's garland of spring,
For only thou hast pearls to spend, old Ocean divine.

All Naiads that from thee had sprung, commanded by thee,
Back to thy Nereid-dances tend, old Ocean divine.

What ships of thought sail forth on thee! Atlantis doth sleep
In silence at thine utmost end, old Ocean divine.

The goblets of the gods, from high Olympus that fall,
Thou dost on coral boughs suspend, old Ocean divine.

A diver in the sea of love my song is, that fain
Thy glory would to all commend, old Ocean divine.

I, like the moon, beneath thy waves with yearning would
    plunge;
Thence might I like the sun ascend, old Ocean divine.

                         RICHARD CHENEVIX TRENCH.

In the Isle of Mull.

THE clouds are gathering in their western dome,
    Deep-drenched with sunlight, as a fleece with dew,
While I with baffled effort still pursue
And track these waters toward their mountain home,—

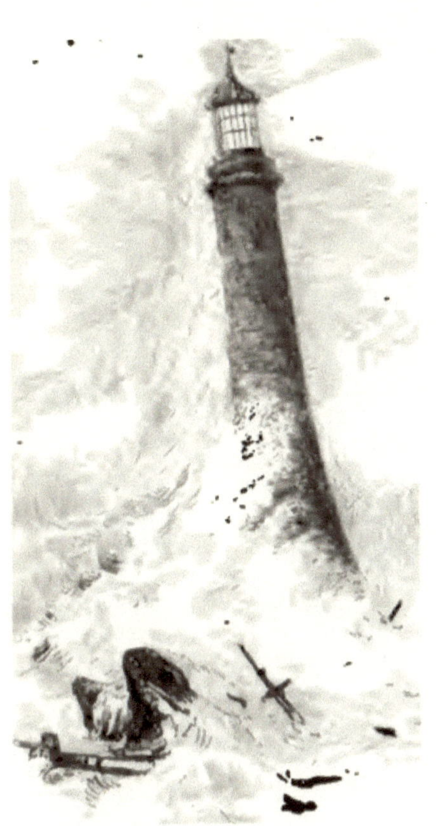

In vain—though cataract, and mimic foam,
And island-spots, round which the streamlet threw
Its sister arms, which joyed to meet anew,
Have lured me on, and won me still to roam ;
Till now, coy nymph, unseen thy waters pass,
Or faintly struggle through the twinkling grass,—
And I, thy springs unvisited, return.
Is it that thou art revelling with thy peers?
Or dost thou feed a solitary urn,
Else unreplenished, with thy own sad tears?

R. C. TRENCH.

THIS winter eve how soft ! how mild !
    How calm the earth ! how calm the sea !
The earth is like a weary child,
    And ocean chants its lullaby.

A little murmur in mine ear !
    A little ripple at my feet !
They only make the silence here,
    Which they disturb not, more complete.

R. C. TRENCH.

The Light-house Girl.

I.

AMID the Channel's wiles and fell decoys
    Where "Casket Beacons" watch the Siren-sea,
A girl was reared who knew nor flower nor tree
Nor breath of grass at dawn, yet had high joys :

The moving lawns whose verdure never cloys
   Were hers.   At last she sailed to Alderney,
   But there she pined.   "*The bustling world,*" said she,
"*Is all too full of trouble and of noise.*"

The storm-child fainting for her home the storm
   Had winds for sponsors—one proud rock for nurse,
   Whose granite arms disperse, and aye disperse
All billowy squadrons tide and wind can form:
No fever of Love she knew, nor Love's alarm:
   The Siren-sea was still her universe.

II.

Love bringeth Fear with eyes of augury:—
   Her lover's boat was out: her ears were dinned
   With sea-sobs warning of the awakened wind
That shook the troubled sun's red canopy.
Even while she prayed the storm's high revelry
   Woke petrel, gull—all revellers wing'd and finn'd—
   And clutch'd a sail brown-patch'd and weather-thinned,
And then a swimmer fought a white wild sea.

"My songs are louder, child, than prayers of thine,"
   The Siren sang: "thy sea-boy waged no strife
   With Hatred's poison, Envy's gangrened knife:—
I strove with him, in deadly sport divine:—
   The old wrestle of the gods for light and life
Was his; then peace within these arms of mine!"

Theodore Watts.

A Morning Swim in Guernsey.

I.

WE are in **the** " Coloured Caves " the sea-maid built ;
  Her walls are stained beyond that lonely fern,
 For she must fly at **every tide's return,**
And all her sea-tints round the walls are spilt.
Outside behold the bay, each headland gilt
  With morning's gold ; far off the foam-wreathes burn
  Like fiery snakes, while here the sweet waves yearn
Up sand more soft **than** Avon's sacred silt.

And smell the sea ! **No breath from wood** or field,
  No scent of **may or** rose or eglantine,
  Cuts off the **old** life where cities suffer and pine,
Shuts the dark house where Memory stands revealed,
Calms the vext spirit, balms a **sorrow unhealed,**
  Like scent of sea-weed rich **of morn and brine.**

II.

As if the Spring's fresh groves should change and shake
  To dark green woods of cedar or terebinth,
  Then break to bloom of amorous hyacinth,
So 'neath us change the waves, rising to take
Each kiss of colour from each cloud and flake
  Round many a rocky hall and labyrinth,
  Where sea-wrought column, arch, and granite plinth,
Show how the sea's fine rage **dares** make and break.

Young with the youth the immortal brine can lend,
  Our glowing limbs, with sea and sun empearled,
Seem born anew, and in your eyes, dear friend,
  Rare pictures shine—like faery flags unfurl'd—
Of Child-land, where the roofs of rainbows bend
  Over the golden wonders of the world.

THEODORE WATTS.

A Coarse Morning.

OH the yellow boisterous sea,
  The surging, chafing, murderous sea !
And the wind-gusts hurtle the torn clouds by,
On to the south through a shuddering sky,
And the bare black ships scud aloof from the land.
  'Tis as like the day as can be,
When the ship came in sight that came never to strand,
The ship that was blown on the sunken sand—
  And he coming back to me !

  Oh the great white snake of foam,
The coiling, writhing snake of white foam,
Hissing and huddering out in the bay,
Over the banks where the wrecked ship lay,
Over the sands where the dead may lie deep !
  There are some in the churchyard loam,
Some two or three the sea flung to our keep :
Their mothers can sit by a grave to weep,
  But *my* son never came home.

AUGUSTA WEBSTER.

On the Shore.

THE angry sunset fades from out the west,
   A glimmering greyness creeps along the sea ;
Wild waves, be hushed, and moan into **your rest,**
   Soon will all earth be sleeping, **why not ye?**

Far off, the heavens **deaden o'er** with sleep,
   The purple twilight darkens on the **hill ;**
Why will ye only ever wake and weep?
   I weary of your sighing, **oh ! be still.**

But ever, ever, moan ye by **the shore,**
   While all your **trouble** surges in **my breast ;**
Oh, waves of **trouble, surge** in me **no more,**
   Or be but still awhile and let me **rest.**

AUGUSTA WEBSTER.

The Flowing Tide.

THE slow green wave comes curling from the **bay,**
   And leaps in spray along the sunny marge,
And steals a little more and more away,
   And drowns the dulse, and lifts the stranded barge.
Leave me, strong tide, my smooth and yellow **shore ;**
But the clear waters deepen more and more :
   Leave me my pathway of the sands, strong tide ;
   Yet are the waves more fair than all they hide.

AUGUSTA WEBSTER.

[*From* The Fisherman.]

NOW, brothers, for the icebergs
   Of frozen Labrador,
Floating spectral in the moonshine,
   Along the low, black shore !
Where like snow the gannet's feathers
   On Brador's rocks are shed,
And the noisy murr are flying,
   Like black scuds, overhead ;

Where in mist the rock is hiding,
   And the sharp reef lurks below,
And the white squall smites in summer,
   And the autumn tempests blow ;
Where, through gray and rolling vapour,
   From evening unto morn,
A thousand boats are hailing,
   Horn answering unto horn. . . .

There we'll drop our lines, and gather
   Old Ocean's treasures in,
Where'er the mottled mackerel
   Turns up a steel-dark fin.
The sea's our field of harvest,
   Its scaly tribes our grain ;
We'll reap the teeming waters
   As at home they reap the plain !

JOHN GREENLEAF WHITTIER.

[*From* The Wreck of Rivermouth.]

RIVERMOUTH Rocks are fair to **see,**
  By dawn or sunset shone across,
When the ebb of the sea has left them free,
  To dry their fringes of gold-green moss :
For there the river comes winding **down**
From salt sea-meadows and uplands brown,
And waves on the outer rocks afoam
Shout to its waters, " Welcome **home !"**

And fair are the sunny isles in **view**
  East **of** the grisly Head of the Boar,
And Agamenticus lifts its blue
  Disk of a cloud the woodlands o'er ;
And southerly, **when the tide is down,**
'Twixt white sea-waves and sand-hills brown,
The beach-birds dance and the gray gulls wheel
Over a floor of burnished steel.

Once, in the old Colonial days,
  Two hundred years ago and more,
A boat sailed down through the winding ways
  Of Hampton River to that low shore,
Full of a goodly company
Sailing out on the summer sea,
Veering to catch the land-breeze light,
With the Boar to left and the Rocks to right. . . .

"Fie on the witch!" cried a merry girl,
 As they rounded the point where Goody Cole
Sat by her door with her wheel atwirl,
 A bent and blear-eyed poor old soul.
"Oho!" she muttered, "ye're brave to-day!
But I hear the little waves laugh and say,
'The broth will be cold that waits at home;
For it's one to go, but another to come!'" . . .

They dropped their lines in the lazy tide,
 Drawing up haddock and mottled cod;
They saw not the Shadow that walked beside,
 They heard not the feet with silence shod.
But thicker and thicker a hot mist grew,
Shot by the lightnings through and through;
And muffled growls, like the growl of a beast,
Ran along the sky from west to east.

Then the skipper looked from the darkening sea
 Up to the dimmed and wading sun;
But he spake like a brave man cheerily,
 "Yet there is time for our homeward run."
Veering and tacking, they backward wore;
And just as a breath from the woods ashore
Blew out to whisper of danger past,
The wrath of the storm came down at last!

The skipper hauled at the heavy sail:
 "God be our help!" he only cried,
As the roaring gale, like the stroke of a flail,
 Smote the boat on its starboard side.

The Shoalsmen looked, but saw **alone**
Dark films of rain-cloud slantwise blown,
Wild rocks lit up by the lightning's glare,
The strife and torment of sea and **air.** . . .

Suddenly seaward **swept the** squall ;
   The low sun smote through **cloudy rack ;**
The Shoals stood **clear in** the light, and all
   The trend of the coast **lay hard and black.**
But far and wide **as** eye could reach,
No life was seen upon wave or beach ;
The boat that went out at morning never
Sailed back again into Hampton River. . . .

O Rivermouth rocks, how sad a sight
   Ye saw in the light of breaking day !
Dead faces looking up cold and white,
   From sand and sea-weed where they lay.
The mad old witch-wife wailed and **wept,**
And cursed the tide as it backward crept :
" Crawl back, crawl back, blue water-snake !
Leave your dead **for** the hearts that break ! "

J. G. WHITTIER.

Part II

RIVER RHYME

[*From* The Boke of Cupide.]

AND the ryver that *then* I sat upon,
   Hit made suche a noyse as hit *ther* ron,
Acordaunt to the foules ermonye,
Me thoght hit was the best*e* melodye
That myght*e* be herd of eny *lyvyng* man.

GEOFFREY CHAUCER.

[*From* Comparison of Love to a Stream

Falling from the Alps.]

FROM these high hills as when a spring doth fall,
   It trilleth down with still and subtle course;
Of this and that it gathers aye, and shall,
Till it have just down flowed to stream, and force,
Then at the foot it rageth over all.

SIR THOMAS WYATT.

[*From* The Faerie Queene, Book ii., Canto v.]

AND fast beside there trickled softly downe
   A gentle streame, whose murmuring wave did play
Emongst the pumy stones, and made a sowne,
   To lull him soft asleepe that by it lay.

EDMUND SPENSER.

[*From* The Faerie Queene, Book iv., Canto xi.]

AND after him the famous rivers came,
   Which doe the earth enrich and beautifie :
The fertile Nile, which creatures new doth frame ;
Long Rhodanus, whose course springs from the skie ;
Faire Ister, flowing from the mountains hie :
Divine Scamander, purpled yet with blood
Of Greeks and Trojans which therein did die ;
Pactolus glistring with his golden flood ;
And Tygris fierce, whose streams of none may be withstood ;

  Great Ganges, and immortall Euphrates
Deepe Indus, and Mæander intricate,
Slow Peneus, and tempestuous Phasides,
Swift Rhene, and Alpheus still immaculate
Ooraxes, feared for great Cyrus fate,
Tybris, renowmed for the Romaines fame,
Rich Oranochy, though but knowen late ;
And that huge River, which doth beare his name
Of warlike Amazons, who doe possesse the same.

Joy on those warlike women, which so **long**
Can from all men so rich a kingdome hold!
And shame on you, O men! which boast your strong
And valiant hearts, **in** thoughts lesse hard and bold,
Yet quaile in conquest of that land of gold.
But this to you, O Britons! **most** pertaines,
To whom the right hereof itselfe hath sold,
The which, for sparing little cost or **paines,**
Loose so immortall glory, and **so endlesse gaines.**

Then **was there** heard a most celestiall sound
Of dainty **musicke,** which did next ensew
Before the **spouse: that was Arion crownd;**
Who, playing on his harpe, unto him drew
The eares and hearts of all that goodly crew,
That even yet the Dolphin, which him bore
Through the Agæan seas from Pirates vew,
Stood still by him astonisht at his **lore,**
And all the raging seas for joy forgot **to rore.**

So went he playing on the watery plaine;
Soone after whom the lovely Bridegroome came,
The noble Thamis, with all his goodly **traine;**
But him before there went, as best became,
His auncient parents, namely th' auncient Thame.
But much more aged was his wife then he,
The Ouze, whom men doe Isis righty name;
Full weake and crooked creature seemed shee,
And almost blind through eld, that scarce her way could see.

Therefore on either side she was sustained
Of two smal grooms, which by their names were hight
The Churne and Charwell, two small streames, which pained
Themselves her footing to direct aright,
Which sayled oft through faint and feeble plight :
But Thame was stronger, and of better stay ;
Yet seem'd full aged by his outward sight,
With head all hoary, and his beard all gray,
Deawed with silver drops that trickled downe alway.

And eke he somewhat seem'd to stoupe afore
With bowed backe, by reason of the lode
And auncient heavy burden which he bore
Of that faire City, wherein make abode
So many learned impes, that shoote abrode,
And with their braunches spred all Britany,
No lesse then do her elder sister's broode.
Joy to you both, ye double noursery
Of Arts ! but, Oxford, thine doth Thame most glorify.

But he their sonne full fresh and jolly was,
All decked in a robe of watchet hew,
On which the waves, glittering like christall glas,
So cunningly enwoven were, that few
Could weenen whether they were false or trew :
And on his head like to a Coronet
He wore, that seemed strange to common vew,
In which were many towres and castels set,
That it encompast round as with a golden fret.

Like as the mother of the Gods, they say,
In her great iron charet wonts to ride,
When to Jove's pallace she doth take her way,
Old Cybele, arayd with pompous pride,
Wearing a Diademe embattild wide
With hundred turrets, like a Turribant;
With such an one was Thamis beautifide;
That was to weet the famous Troynovant,
In which her kingdomes throne is chiefly resiant.

And round about him many a **pretty Page**
Attended duely, ready to obay;
All little Rivers which owe vassallage
To him, as to their Lord, and tribute pay:
The chaulky Kenet, and the Thetis gray,
The morish Cole, and the soft sliding Breane,
The wanton Lee, that oft doth loose his **way;**
And the still Darent, in whose waters cleane
Ten thousand fishes play and decke his pleasant streame.

Then came his neighbour flouds which nigh him dwell,
And water all the English soile throughout:
They all on him this day attended well,
And with meet service waited him about,
Ne none disdained low to him to lout:
No, not the stately Severne grudg'd at all,
Ne storming Humber, though he looked stout;
But both him honor'd as their principall,
And let their swelling waters low before him fall.

There was the speedy Tamar, which devides
The Cornish and the Devonish confines ;
Through both whose borders swiftly downe it glides,
And, meeting Plim, to Plimmouth thence declines :
And Dart, nigh chockt with sands of tinny mines.
But Avon marched in more stately path,
Proud of his Adamants with which he shines
And glisters wide, as als' of wondrous Bath,
And Bristow faire, which on his waves he builded hath.

And there came Stoure with terrible aspect,
Bearing his six deformed heads on hye,
That doth his course through Blandford plains direct,
And washeth Winborne meades in season drye.
Next him went Wylibourne with passage slye,
That of his wylinesse his name doth take,
And of him selfe doth name the shire thereby :
And Mole, that like a nousling Mole doth make
His way still under ground, till Thamis he overtake.

Then came the Rother, decked all with woods
Like a wood God, and flowing fast to Rhy;
And Sture, that parteth with his pleasant floods
The Easterne Saxons from the Southerne ny,
And Clare and Harwitch both doth beautify :
Him follow'd Yar, soft washing Norwitch wall,
And with him brought a present joyfully
Of his owne fish unto their festivall,
Whose like none else could shew, the which the Ruffins call.

Next these the plenteous Ouse came far from land,
By many a city and by many a towne
And many rivers taking under-hand
Into his waters as he passeth downe,
The Cle, the Were, the Grant, the Sture, the Rowne,
Thence doth by Huntingdon and Cambridge flit,
My mother Cambridge, whom as with a crowne
He doth adorne, and is adorn'd of it
With many a gentle Muse and many a learned wit.

And after him the fatall Welland went,
That, if old sawes prove true (which God forbid !)
Shall drowne all Holland with his excrement,
And shall see Stamford, though now homely hid,
Then shine in learning, more then ever did
Cambridge or Oxford, Englands goodly beames.
And next to him the Nene downe softly slid ;
And beauteous Trent, that in him self enseames
Both thirty sorts of fish, and thirty sundry streames.

Next these came Tyne, along whose stony bancke
That Romaine monarch built a brasen wall,
Which mote the feebled Briton's strongly flancke
Against the Picts that swarmed over-all.
Which yet thereof Gualsever they doe call :
And Twede, the limit betwixt Logris land
And Albany : and Eden, though but small,
Yet often stainde with bloud of many a band
Of Scots and English both, that tyned on his strand.

Then came those sixe sad brethren, like forlorne,
That whilome were (as antique fathers tell)
Sixe valiant Knights of one faire Nymphe yborne,
Which did in noble deedes of armes excell,
And wonned there where now Yorke people dwell ;
Still Ure, swift Werfe and Oze the most of might,
High Swale, unquiet Nide, and troublous Skell ;
All whom a Scythian king, that Humber hight,
Slew cruelly, and in the river drowned quight.

But past not long ere Brutus warlicke sonne,
Locrinus, them aveng'd, and the same date,
Which the proud Humber unto them had donne,
By equall dome repayed on his owne pate :
For in the selfe same river, where he late
Had drenched them, he drowned him againe,
And nam'd the river of his wretched fate
Whose bad condition yet it doth retaine,
Oft tossed with his stormes which therein still remaine.

These after came the stony shallow Lone,
That to old Loncaster his name doth lend ;
And following Dee, which Britons long ygone
Did call divine, that doth by Chester tend ;
And Conway, which out of his streame doth send
Plenty of pearles to decke his dames withall ;
And Lindus that his pikes doth most commend,
Of which the auncient Lincolne men doe call :
All these together marched toward Proteus hall.

Ne thence the Irishe Rivers absent were,
Sith no lesse famous than the rest they bee,
And joyne in neighbourhood of Kingdome nere,
Why should they not likewise **in** love agree,
And joy likewise the solemne day to see?
They saw it all, and present were in place;
Though I them all according their **degree**
Cannot recount nor tell their hidden race,
Nor read the salvage **cuntreis.thorough which they pace.**

There was the **Liffy** rolling downe the lea,
The sandy Slane, the stony Aubrian,
The spacious Shenan spreading like a **sea,**
The pleasant Boyne, **the** fishy fruitfull Ban,
Swift Awniduff, **which** of the English **man**
Is cal'de Blacke-water, and the Liffar **deep,**
Sad Trowis, that once his people over-ran,
Strong Allo tombling **from Slewlogher** steep,
And Mulla mine, whose waves I **whilom taught to weep.**

And there the three **renowmed** brethren were,
Which that great Gyant Blomius **begot**
Of the faire Nimph Rheusa wandring there.
One day, as she to shunne the season **whot**
Under Slewboome in shady grove was got,
This Gyant found her and by force deflowr'd;
Whereof conceiving, she in time forth brought
These three faire sons, which being thenceforth powrd
In three great rivers ran, and many countreis scowrd.

The first the gentle Shure that, making way
By sweet Clonmell, adornes rich Waterford;
The next, the stubborne Newre whose waters gray,
By faire Kilkenny and Rossepontè boord;
The third, the goodly Barow which doth hoord
Great heapes of salmons in his deepe bosome:
All which, long sundred, doe at last accord
To joyne in one, ere to the sea they come;
So, flowing all from one, all one at last become.

There also was the wide embayed Mayre;
The pleasaunt Bandon crownd with many a wood;
The spreading Lee that, like an Island fayre,
Encloseth Corke with his devided flood;
And balefull Oure, late staind with English blood,
With many more whose names no tongue can tell;
All which that day in order seemly good,
Did on the Thamis attend, and waited well
To doe their dueful service, as to them befell.

SPENSER.

[*From* Ovid's Banquet of Sense.]

FORWARD and back and forward went he thus,
   Like wanton Thamysis that hastes to greet
The brackish court of old Oceanus;
And as by London's bosom she doth fleet,
  Casts herself proudly through the bridge's twists,
Where, as she takes again her crystal feet,
  She curls her silver hair like amourists,

Smoothes her bright cheeks, adorns her **brow with ships,**
And, empress-like, along the **coast she trips.**

Till **coming near the sea, she hears him roar,**
Tumbling her churlish billows in her face,
Then, more dismay'd than insolent before,
Charged to rough battle for **his smooth embrace,**
  She croucheth **close within her winding banks,**
And creeps retreat into her peaceful palace;
  Yet straight high-flowing in **her female pranks**
Again she will be wanton, and again,
By no means staid, nor able to contain.

GEORGE CHAPMAN.

[*From* Idea, 53.]

CLEAR ANKER, on whose silver-sanded shore
    My soul-shrined saint, my fair Idea, lies;
O blessèd Brook, whose **milk-white swans adore**
    Thy crystal stream, refinèd **by her eyes,**
Where sweet myrrh-breathing Zephyr in **the Spring**
    Gently distils his nectar-drooping **showers,**
Where nightingales in Arden sit and **sing**
    Amongst the dainty dew-impearlèd flowers;
Say thus, fair Brook, when thou shalt see thy queen,—
    " Lo, here thy shepherd spent his wand'ring years,
And in these shades, dear nymph, he oft hath been,
    And here to thee **he** sacrificed his tears."
      Fair **Arden, thou** my Tempe art alone,
      And **thou,** sweet Anker, art my Helicon.

MICHAEL DRAYTON.

M

[*From* King John, Act iii., Scene i.]

WHY holds thine eye that lamentable rheum,
    Like a proud river peering o'er his bounds?
WILLIAM SHAKESPEARE.

[*From* King Richard II., Act iii., Scene ii.]

AN unseasonable stormy day,
    Which makes the silver rivers drown their shores,
As if the world were all dissolv'd to tears.
SHAKESPEARE.

[*From* King Henry IV., Part I., Act iii., Scene i.]

HOTSPUR. Methinks my moiety, north from Burton here,
In quantity equals not one of yours :
See how this river comes me cranking in,
And cuts me from the best of all my land
A huge half-moon, a monstrous cantle out.
I'll have the current in this place damm'd up,
And here the smug and silver Trent shall run
In a new channel, fair and evenly :
It shall not wind with such a deep indent,
To rob me of so rich a bottom here.

Glendower. Not wind ! it shall, it must; you see it doth.
Mortimer. Yea, but
Mark how he bears his course, and runs me up
With like advantage on the other side ;
Gelding the opposéd continent as much
As on the other side it takes from you.
    Worcester. Yea, but a little charge will trench him here,
And on this north side win this cape of land ;
And then he runs straight and even.

SHAKESPEARE.

[*From* The Two Gentlemen of Verona, Act ii., Scene vii.]

THE current, that with gentle murmur glides,
    Thou know'st, being stopp'd, impatiently doth rage ;
But, when his fair course is not hindered,
He makes sweet music with the enamell'd stones,
Giving a gentle kiss to every sedge
He overtaketh in his pilgrimage ;
And so by many winding nooks he strays,
With willing sport to the wild ocean.

SHAKESPEARE.

[*From* Othello, Act iv., Scene iii.]

THE fresh streams ran by her, and murmur'd her moans.

SHAKESPEARE.

[*From* The False One, Act iii., Scene iv.]

*L*ABOURERS. Come, let us help the reverend Nile;
      He's very old; alas the while!
Let us dig him easy ways,
And prepare a thousand plays:
To delight his streams let's sing
A loud welcome to our spring;
This way let his curling heads
Fall into our new-made beds;
This way let his wanton spawns
Frisk, and glide it o'er the lawns.
This way profit comes, and gain:
How he tumbles here amain!
How his waters hasté to fall
Into our channels!   Labour, all,
And let him in; let Nilus flow,
And perpetual plenty shew.
With incense let us bless the brim,
And as the wanton fishes swim,
Let us gums and garlands fling,
And loud our timbrels ring.
   Come, old father, come away!
   Our labour is our holiday.
                    Enter Nilus.
   Isis. Here comes the agèd River now,
With garlands of great pearl his brow
Begirt and rounded.   In his flow
All things take life, and all things grow.

A thousand wealthy treasures still,
To do him service at his will,
Follow his rising flood, and pour
Perpetual blessings in our store.
Hear him ; and next there will advance
His sacred heads, to tread a dance
In honour of my royal guest :
Mark them too ; and you have a feast.
    Nilus. Make room for my rich waters' fall,
      And bless my flood ;
Nilus comes flowing to you all
      Encrease and good.
Now the plants and flowers shall spring,
And the merry ploughman sing.
In my hidden waves I bring
Bread, and wine, and every thing.
Let the damsels sing me in,
  Sing aloud, that I may rise :
Your holy feasts and hours begin,
  And each hand bring a sacrifice.
Now thy wanton pearls I shew,
That to ladies' fair necks grow ;
     Now my gold,
  And treasures that can ne'er be told,
Shall bless this land, by my rich flow,
And after this, to crown your eyes,
My hidden holy head arise.

             BEAUMONT AND FLETCHER.

[*From* The Faithful Shepherdess, Act iii., Scene i.]

AMORET. Who hath restor'd my sense, given me new
  breath,
And brought me back out of the arms of death?
 River God. I have heal'd thy wounds.
 Amoret. Ah me !
 River God. Fear not him that succour'd thee.
I am this fountain's god ; below,
My waters to a river grow,
And 'twixt two banks with osiers set,
That only prosper in the wet,
Through the meadows do they glide,
Wheeling still on every side,
Sometimes winding round about,
To find the evenest channel out.
And if thou wilt go with me,
Leaving mortal company,
In the cool streams shalt thou lie,
Free from harm as well as I :
I will give thee for thy food
No fish that useth in the mud ;
But trout and pike that love to swim
Where the gravel from the brim
Through the pure streams may be seen :
Orient pearl, fit for a queen,
Will I give thy love to win,
And a shell to keep them in :

Not a fish in all my brook
That shall disobey thy look,
But, when thou wilt, come sliding by,
  And from thy white hand take a fly.
And to make thee understand,
How I can my waves command,
They shall bubble whilst **I sing,**
Sweeter than **the silver spring.**

John Fletcher.

[*From* The Pilgrim, Act iii.]

DOWN, ye angry waters all !
    Ye loud whistling whirlwinds, fall !
Down, ye proud waves ! ye storms, cease !
I command ye, be at peace !
Fright not with your **churlish notes,**
Nor bruise the keel of bark **that floats ;**
No devouring fish come nigh,
Nor monster in my empery
Once show his head, or terror bring ;
But let the weary sailor sing :
Amphitrite, with white arms,
Strike my lute, I'll sing [thy] **charms.**

Fletcher.

[*From* The River of Forth Feasting.]

AND you my nymphs, rise from your moist repair;
 Strew all your springs and grots with lilies fair :
Some swiftest-footed, get them hence and pray
Our floods and lakes come keep this holiday ;
Whate'er beneath Albania's hills do run,
Which see the rising or the setting sun,
Which drink stern Grampius' mists or Ochill's snows ;
Stone-rolling Tay, Tyne tortoise-like that flows,
The pearly Don, the Dee, the fertile Spey,
Wild Nevern which doth see our longest day ;
Ness smoking sulphur, Leave with mountains crowned,
Strange Lomond for his floating isles renown'd,
The Irish Rian, Ken, the silver Air,
The snaky Dun, the Ore with rushy hair,
The crystal-streaming Nid, loud-bellowing Clyde,
Tweed, which no more our kingdoms shall divide ;
Rank-swelling Annan, Lid with curled streams,
The Esks, the Solway, where they lose their names ;
To every one proclaim our joys and feasts,
Our triumphs, bid all come, and be our guests ;
And as they meet in Neptune's azure hall,
Bid them bid sea-gods keep this festival.

WILLIAM DRUMMOND.

[His Tears to Thamesis.]

I SEND, I send here my supremest kiss,
   To thee, my silver-footed Thamesis ;
No more shall I reiterate thy strand,
Whereon so many stately structures stand :
Nor in the summer's sweeter evenings go,
To bathe in thee, as thousand others do :
No more shall I along thy chrystal glide,
In barge, with boughs and rushes beautified,
With soft-smooth virgins for our chaste disport,
To Richmond, Kingston, and to Hampton-Court :
Never again shall I with finny oar
Put from or draw unto the faithful shore,
And landing here, or safely landing there,
Make way to my beloved Westminster,
Or to the golden Cheap-side, where the earth
Of Julia Herrick gave to me my birth.
May all clean nymphs and curious water dames
With swan-like state float up and down thy streams ;
No drought upon thy wanton waters fall
To make them lean, and languishing at all :
No ruffling winds come hither to disease
Thy pure and silver-wristed Naiades.
Keep up your state, ye streams ; and as ye spring,
Never make sick your banks by surfeiting.
Grow young with tides, and though I see ye never,
Receive this vow ; so fare ye well for ever.

ROBERT HERRICK.

[*From* To Phillis.]

THE silver-shedding streams
   Shall gently melt thee into dreams.

HERRICK.

[*From* Paradise Lost, Book iv.]

SOUTHWARD through Eden went a river large,
   Nor changed his course, but through the shaggy hill
Passed underneath ingulfed ; for God had thrown
That mountain, as his garden-mould, high raised
Upon the rapid current, which, through veins
Of porous earth with kindly thirst up-drawn,
Rose a fresh fountain, and with many a rill
Watered the garden ; thence united fell
Down the steep glade, and met the nether flood,
Which from his darksome passage now appears,
And now, divided into four main streams,
Runs diverse, wandering many a famous realm
And country whereof here needs no account ;
But rather to tell how, if Art could tell
How, from that sapphire fount the crispèd brooks,
Rolling on orient pearl and sands of gold,
With mazy error under pendent shades
Ran nectar, visiting each plant, and fed
Flowers worthy of Paradise.

JOHN MILTON.

[*From* Paradise Lost, Book viii.]

ABOUT me round I saw . . .
Liquid lapse of murmuring streams.

MILTON.

[*From* A Vacation Exercise.]

RIVERS, arise : whether **thou** be the son
Of utmost Tweed, **or** Ouse, or gulfy Dun,
Or Trent, who, **like** some earth-born giant, **spreads**
His thirty arms along the indented **meads,**
Or sullen Mole, that runneth underneath,
Or Severn swift, guilty **of maiden's death,**
Or rocky **Avon, or of sedgy Lea,**
Or coaly Tyne, **or ancient hallowed Dee,**
Or Humber loud, **that keeps the Scythian's name,**
Or Medway **smooth, or royal-towered Thame.**

MILTON.

[*From* Cooper's Hill.]

MY eye, descending from the Hill, surveys
Where Thames amongst the wanton valleys strays ;
Thames, the most loved of all the Ocean's sons,
By his old sire, to his embraces runs,
Hasting to pay his tribute to the sea,
Like mortal life to meet eternity ;

Though with those streams he no resemblance hold,
Whose foam is amber, and their gravel gold,
His genuine and less guilty wealth t' explore,
Search not his bottom, but survey his shore,
O'er which he kindly spreads his spacious wing,
And hatches plenty for th' ensuing spring ;
Nor then destroys it with too fond a stay,
Like mothers which their infants overlay ;
Nor, with a sudden and impetuous wave,
Like profuse kings, resumes the wealth he gave ;
No unexpected inundations spoil
The mower's hopes, nor mock the ploughman's toil :
But godlike his unwearied bounty flows,
First loves to do, then loves the good he does ;
Nor are his blessings to his banks confin'd,
But free and common as the sea or wind ;
When he, to boast or to disperse his stores,
Full of the tributes of his grateful shores,
Visits the world, and in his flying tow'rs,
Brings home to us, and makes both Indies ours,
Finds wealth where 'tis, bestows it where it wants,
Cities in deserts, woods in cities, plants ;
So that to us no thing, no place is strange,
While his fair bosom is the world's exchange.
O could I flow like thee, and make thy stream
My great example, as it is my theme !
Though deep, yet clear, though gentle, yet not dull,
Strong without rage, without o'erflowing full.

Sir John Denham.

[*From* Wealth, or the Woody.]

LIKE *Nilus* swelling frae his unkend Head,
    Frae Bank to Brae o'erflows ilk Rig and Mead,
Instilling lib'ral store of genial sap,
Whence sun-burn'd Gypsies reap a plenteous Crap:
Thus flows our sea, but with this Diff'rence wide,
But ance a Year their River heaves his Tide;
Ours aft ilk Day t' enrich the Common Weal,
Bangs o'er its Banks, and dings Ægyptian Nile.

ALLAN RAMSAY.

To the River Lodon.

AH! what a weary race my feet have run,
    Since first I trod thy banks with alders crown'd,
And thought my way was all through fairy ground,
Beneath thy azure sky, and golden sun:
Where first my Muse to lisp her notes begun!
While pensive Memory traces back the round,
Which fills the varied interval between;
Much pleasure, more of sorrow, marks the scene.
Sweet native stream! those skies and suns so pure
No more return, to cheer my evening road!
Yet still one joy remains, that not obscure,
Nor useless, all my vacant days have flow'd,
From youth's gay dawn to manhood's prime mature;
Nor with the Muse's laurel unbestowed.

THOMAS WARTON.

[*From* Windsor Forest.]

ABOVE the rest a rural nymph was fam'd,
    Thy offspring, Thames! the fair Ladona named.

.   .   .   .

Faint, breathless, thus she pray'd, nor pray'd in vain;
"Ah, Cynthia! ah—tho' banish'd from thy train,
Let me, O let me, to the shades repair,
My native shades—there weep, and murmur there."
She said, and melting as in tears she lay,
In a soft, silver stream dissolv'd away.
The silver stream her virgin coldness keeps,
For ever murmurs, and for ever weeps;
Still bears the name the hapless virgin bore,
And bathes the forest where she rang'd before.
In her chaste current oft the goddess laves,
And with celestial tears augments the waves.
Oft in her glass the musing shepherd spies
The headlong mountains and the downward skies,
The wat'ry landscape of the pendant-woods,
And absent trees that tremble in the floods;
In the clear azure gleam, the flocks are seen,
And floating forests paint the waves with green,
Thro' the fair scene roll slow the lingering streams,
Then foaming pour along, and rush into the Thames.
    Thou, too, great father of the British floods!
With joyful pride survey'st our lofty woods;
Where tow'ring oaks their growing honours rear,
And future navies on thy shores appear.

Not Neptune's self from **all her streams receives**
A wealthier tribute than to thine **he** gives.
No seas so rich, so gay no banks appear,
No lake so gentle, and no spring so clear.
Nor Po so swells the fabling Poet's lays,
While led along the skies his current **strays,**
As thine, which visits Windsor's fam'd abodes
To grace the mansion of our earthly **Gods :**
Nor all his stars above a lustre show,
Like the bright Beauties on thy banks below,
Where Jove, subdued by mortal Passion still,
Might change Olympus for a nobler hill.

ALEXANDER POPE.

[*From* Windsor Forest.]

IN that blest moment **from his oozy bed**
    Old Father Thames advanc'd **his reverend head.**
His tresses dropp'd with dews, and o'er the stream
His shining horns diffus'd a golden gleam :
Grav'd on his urn appear'd the moon, that guides
His swelling waters and alternate tides ;
The figur'd **streams in waves of** silver roll'd,
And on their banks Augusta rose in gold.
Around his throne the sea-born brothers stood,
Who swell with tributary urns his flood ;
First **the** fam'd authors of his ancient name,
The winding Isis, and the fruitful Thame :
The Kennet swift, **for** silver eels renown'd ;

The Loddon slow, with verdant alders crown'd ;
Cole, whose dark streams his flowery islands lave ;
And chalky Wey, that rolls a milky wave :
The blue, transparent Vandalis appears ;
The gulfy Lee his sedgy tresses rears ;
And sullen Mole, that hides his diving flood ;
And silent Darent, stain'd with Danish blood.
    High in the midst, upon his urn reclin'd
(His sea-green mantle waving with the wind),
The god appear'd : he turn'd his azure eyes
Where Windsor-domes and pompous turrets rise ;
Then bow'd and spoke ; the winds forget to roar,
And the hush'd waves glide softly to the shore.
    Hail, sacred peace ! hail, long-expected days,
That Thames's glory to the skies shall raise !
Tho' Tiber's streams immortal Rome behold,
Tho' foaming Hermus swells with tides of gold,
From heav'n itself though sev'nfold Nilus flows,
And harvests on a hundred realms bestows ;
These now no more shall be the Muse's themes,
Lost in my fame, as in the sea their streams.
Let Volga's banks with iron squadrons shine,
And groves of lances glitter on the Rhine,
Let barb'rous Ganges arm a servile train ;
Be mine the blessings of a peaceful reign.
No more my sons shall dye with British blood
Red Iber's sands, or Ister's foaming flood :
Safe on my shore each unmolested swain
Shall tend the flocks, or reap the bearded grain.

     .   .   .   .

The time shall come, when, free as seas or wind,
Unbounded Thames shall flow for all mankind,
Whole nations enter with each swelling **tide,**
And seas but join the regions they divide ;
Earth's distant ends our glory shall behold,
And the new world launch **forth to seek the old.**

POPE.

[*From* Pastorals—Spring.]

O'ER golden sands let rich Pactolus flow,
    And trees weep amber **on the banks of Po ;**
Blest Thames's shores the brightest **beauties yield,**
Feed here my lambs, I'll seek **no distant field.**

POPE.

[*From* The Fleece, Book iii.]

THROUGH **Tyne,** and Tees,
    Through Weare, and Lune, and merchandizing Hull,
And Swale, and Aire, whose crystal waves reflect
The various colours of the tinctur'd **web ;**
Through **Ken,** swift rolling down his rocky dale,
Like giddy youth impetuous, then at Wick
Curbing his train, and, with the sober pace
Of cautious Eld, meandering to the deep ;
Through Dart, and sullen Exe, whose murmuring wave
Envies the Dune and Rother, who have won

N

The serge and **kersie to their blanching** streams;
Through Towy, winding under Merlin's towers,
And Usk, that frequent, among hoary rocks,
On her deep waters paints th' impending scene,
Wild torrents, craggs, and woods, and mountain **snows.**

JOHN DYER.

[*From* The Seasons—Autumn.]

THEN Commerce brought into **the public walk**
  The busy merchant; . . . . . .
. . . . . . and thy stream, O Thames,
Large, gentle, deep, majestic, king of floods!
Chose for his grand resort. On either hand,
Like a long wintry forest, groves of masts
Shot up their spires; the bellying sheet between
Possessed the breezy **void**; the sooty hulk
Steer'd sluggish **on**; the splendid barge **along**
Row'd regular, **to** harmony; around,
The boat, light-skimming, stretched **its oary** wings;
While deep the various voice of fervent toil
From bank to bank increased.

JAMES THOMSON.

[*From* The Seasons—Winter.]

WIDE o'er the brim, with many a torrent swelled,
  And the mixed ruin of its banks o'erspread,
At last the rous'd-up river pours along:

Resistless, roaring, dreadful, down it comes,
From the rude mountain, and the mossy wild,
Tumbling through rocks abrupt, and sounding far ;
Then o'er the sanded **valley floating spreads,**
Calm, sluggish, silent ; till again, constrained
Between two meeting hills, it **bursts away,**
Where rocks **and woods o'erhang the turbid stream ;**
There gathering triple force, **rapid, and deep,**
It boils, and wheels, **and foams, and thunders through.**

THOMSON.

[*From* The Pleasures of Imagination, Book ii.]

WE view,
Amid the noontide walk, a limpid rill
Gush **through the trickling herbage, to the thirst**
Of summer, yielding the **delicious draught**
Of cool refreshment ; o'er the **mossy brink**
Shines not the surface clearer, and the waves
With sweeter music murmur as they flow ?

MARK AKENSIDE.

[*From* Ode to Leven-Water.]

PURE stream ! in whose transparent wave
My youthful limbs I wont to lave ;
No torrents stain thy limpid source,
No rocks impede thy dimpling course,

That sweetly warbles o'er its bed,
With white, round, polish'd pebbles spread ;
While, lightly poised, the scaly brood
In myriads cleave thy crystal flood ;
The springing trout in speckled pride ;
The salmon, monarch of the tide ;
The ruthless pike, intent on war ;
The silver eel, and mottled par.
Devolving from thy parent lake,
A charming maze thy waters make,
By bowers of birch, and groves of pine,
And edges flower'd with eglantine.

     TOBIAS GEORGE SMOLLETT.

[*From* Love Poem—Written in a Quarrel.]

SEE where the Thames, the purest stream
 That wavers to the noon-day beam,
  Divides the vale below ;
While like a vein of liquid ore
His waves enrich the happy shore,
  Still shining as they flow !

Nor yet, my Delia, to the main
Runs the sweet tide without a stain,
  Unsullied as it seems ;
The nymphs of many a sable flood
Deform with streaks of oozy mud
  The bosom of the Thames.

Some idle rivulets, that feed
And suckle every noisome weed,
   A sandy bottom boast ;
For ever bright, for ever clear,
The trifling shallow rills appear
   In their own channel lost.

Thus fares it with the human soul,
Where copious floods of passion roll,
   By genuine love supplied ;
Fair in itself the current shows,
But ah ! a thousand anxious woes
   Pollute the noble tide.

WILLIAM COWPER.

A Comparison.

THE lapse of time and rivers is the same,
   Both speed their journey with a restless stream ;
The silent pace with which they steal away,
No wealth can bribe, no prayers persuade to stay ;
Alike irrevocable both when past,
And a wide ocean swallows both at last.
Though each resemble each in every part,
A difference strikes at length the musing heart ;
Streams never flow in vain ; where streams abound
How laughs the land with various plenty crowned !
But time, that should enrich the nobler mind,
Neglected, leaves a dreary waste behind.

COWPER.

To the River Arun.

BE the proud Thames of trade the busy mart !
    Arun, to thee will other praise belong !
Dear to the lover's and the mourner's heart,
And ever sacred to the sons of song !
Thy banks romantic hopeless Love shall seek,
Where o'er the rocks the mantling bindweed flaunts ;
And Sorrow's drooping form and faded cheek
Choose on thy willow'd shore her lonely haunts.
Banks, which inspired thy Otway's plaintive strain !
Wilds, whose lorn echoes learned the deeper tone
Of Collins' powerful shell ! yet once again
Another poet—Hayley—is thine own !
Thy classic stream anew shall hear a lay,
Bright as its waves, and various as its way.

CHARLOTTE SMITH.

[*From* Clifton.]

THE yellow Avon, creeping at my side,
    In sullen billows rolls a muddy tide ;
No sportive Naiads on her streams are seen,
No cheerful pastimes deck the gloomy scene ;
Fix'd in a stupor by the cheerless plain,
For fairy flights the fancy toils in vain ;
For though her waves, by commerce richly blest,
Roll to her shores the treasures of the west,

Though her broad banks trade's busy aspect wears,
She seems unconscious of the wealth she bears.

THOMAS CHATTERTON.

[*From* The Death of Nicou.]

ON Tiber's banks, Tiber, whose waters glide
  In slow meanders down to Gaigra's side;
And, circling all the horrid mountain round,
Rushes impetuous to the deep profound;
Rolls o'er the ragged rocks with hideous yell;
Collects its waves beneath the earth's vast shell:
There for awhile, in loud confusion hurled,
It crumbles mountains down, and shakes the world,
Till, borne upon the pinions of the air,
Through the rent earth the bursting waves appear;
Fiercely propell'd, the whiten'd billows rise,
Break from the cavern and ascend the skies:
Then lost and conquered by superior force,
Through hot Arabia holds its rapid course.

CHATTERTON.

The Banks of Nith.

THE Thames flows proudly to the sea,
  Where royal cities stately stand;
But sweeter flows the Nith to me,
  Where Cummins ance had high command:
When shall I see that honour'd land,
  That winding stream I love so dear!

Must wayward fortune's adverse hand
　　For ever, ever keep me here?

How lovely, Nith, thy fruitful vales,
　　Where spreading hawthorns gaily bloom;
How sweetly wind thy sloping dales,
　　Where lambkins wanton thro' the broom!
Tho' wandering, now, must be my doom,
　　Far from thy bonie banks and braes,
May there my latest hours consume,
　　Amang the friends of early days!

ROBERT BURNS.

[*From* Afton Water.]

HOW lofty, sweet Afton, thy neighbouring hills,
　　Far mark'd with the courses of clear, winding rills;
There daily I wander as noon rises high,
My flocks and my Mary's sweet cot in my eye.

How pleasant thy banks and green valleys below,
Where wild in the woodlands the primroses blow;
There oft as mild ev'ning weeps over the lea,
The sweet-scented birk shades my Mary and me.

Thy crystal stream, Afton, how lovely it glides,
And winds by the cot where my Mary resides;
How wanton thy waters her snowy feet lave,
As gathering sweet flow'rets she stems thy clear wave.

BURNS.

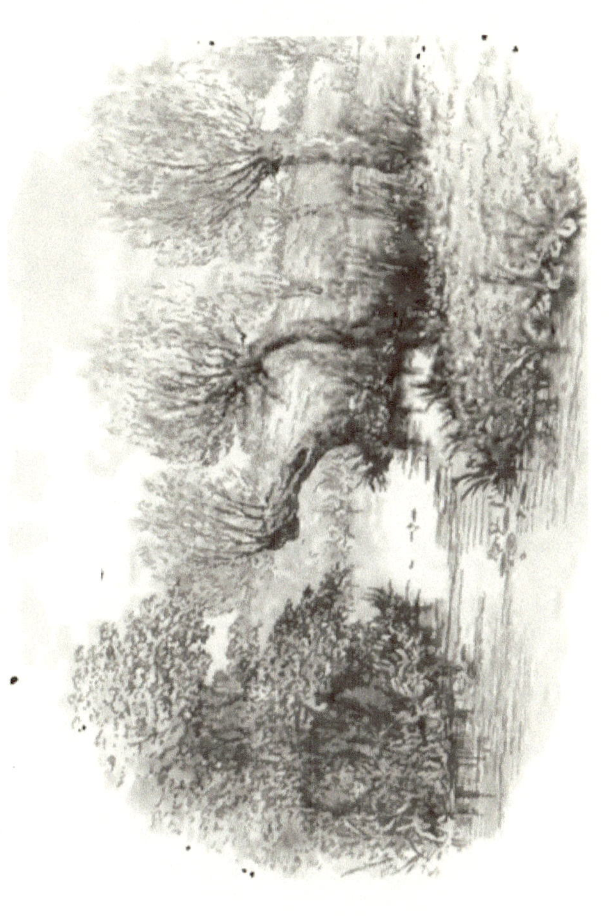

The Tweed Visited.

O TWEED ! a stranger, that with **wandering feet**
  O'er hill and dale has journeyed **many a mile,**
(If so his weary thoughts he might beguile),
Delighted turns thy stranger-stream to greet.
The **waving** branches that romantic bend
  O'er thy tall banks, a soothing charm bestow ;
  The murmurs of thy wandering wave below
Seem like the converse of some long-lost friend.
Delightful stream ! though now along thy shore,
  When spring returns in all her wonted pride,
The distant pastoral pipe is heard no **more ;**
  Yet here while laverocks **sing could I abide,**
Far from the stormy world's **contentious roar,**
  To muse upon thy banks **at eventide.**

WILLIAM LISLE BOWLES.

Yarrow Unvisited.

FROM Stirling Castle we had seen
  The mazy Forth unravelled ;
Had trod the banks of Clyde, and Tay,
And with the Tweed had travelled ;
And when **we** came to Clovenford,
Then said my " *Winsome Marrow* "
" Whate'er betide, we'll turn aside,
And see the Braes of Yarrow."

"Let Yarrow folk, *frae* Selkirk town,
Who have been buying, selling,
Go back to Yarrow, 'tis their own ;
Each maiden to her dwelling !
On Yarrow's banks let herons feed,
Hares couch, and rabbits burrow !
But we will downward with the Tweed,
Nor turn aside to Yarrow.

There's Galla Water, Leader Haughs,
Both lying right before us ;
And Dryborough, where with chiming Tweed,
The lint-whites sing in chorus ;
There's pleasant Teviot-dale, a land
Made blithe with plough and harrow ;
Why throw away a needful day
To go in search of Yarrow ?

What's Yarrow but a river bare,
That glides the dark hills under ?
There are a thousand such elsewhere,
As worthy of your wonder."
—Strange words they seemed of slight and scorn ;
My true love sighed for sorrow ;
And looked me in the face, to think,
I thus could speak of Yarrow !

"Oh ! green," said I, "are Yarrow's holms,
And sweet is Yarrow flowing !
Fair hangs the apple frae the rock,
But we will leave it growing.

O'er hilly path, and open strath,
We'll wander Scotland thorough;
But, though so near, we will not turn
Unto the dale of Yarrow.

Let beeves and home-bred kine partake,
The sweets of Burn-mill meadow;
The swan on still St Mary's Lake,
Float double, swan and shadow!
We will not see them; will not go,
To-day, nor yet to-morrow;
Enough if in our hearts we know
There's such a place as Yarrow.

Be Yarrow stream unseen, unknown!
It must, or we shall rue it:
We have a vision of our own;
Ah! why should we undo it?
The treasured dreams of times long past
We'll keep them, winsome Marrow!
For when we're there, although 'tis fair,
'Twill be another Yarrow!

If Care with freezing years should come,
And wandering seem but folly,—
Should we be loth to stir from home,
And yet be melancholy;
Should life be dull, and spirits low,
'Twill soothe us in our sorrow
That earth has something yet to show,
The bonny holms of Yarrow.

WILLIAM WORDSWORTH.

Yarrow Revisited.

September 1814.

AND is this—Yarrow?—*This* the Stream
  Of which my fancy cherished,
So faithfully, a waking dream?
  An image that hath perished!
O that some Minstrel's harp were near,
  To utter notes of gladness,
And chase this silence from the air,
  That fills my heart with sadness!

Yet why?—a silvery current flows
  With uncontrolled meanderings;
Nor have these eyes by greener hills
  Been soothed, in all my wanderings.
And, through her depths, Saint Mary's Lake
  Is visibly delighted;
For not a feature of those hills
  Is in the mirror slighted.

A blue sky bends o'er Yarrow vale,
  Save where that pearly whiteness
Is round the rising sun diffused,
  A tender hazy brightness;
Mild dawn of promise! that includes
  All profitless dejection;
Though not unwilling here to admit
  A pensive recollection.

Where was it that the famous Flower
  Of Yarrow Vale lay bleeding?
His bed perchance was yon smooth mound
  On which the herd is feeding:
And haply from this crystal pool,
  Now peaceful as the morning,
The Water-wraith ascended thrice—
  And gave his doleful warning.

Delicious is the Lay that sings
  The haunts of happy Lovers,
The path that leads them to the grove,
  The leafy grove that covers:
And Pity sanctifies the Verse
  That paints, by strength of sorrow,
The unconquerable strength of love;
  Bear witness, rueful Yarrow!

But thou, that didst appear so fair
  To fond imagination,
Dost rival in the light of day
  Her delicate creation:
Meek loveliness is round thee spread,
  A softness still and holy;
The grace of forest charms decayed,
  And pastoral melancholy.

That region left, the vale unfolds
  Rich groves of lofty stature,
With Yarrow winding through the pomp
  Of cultivated nature;

And, rising from those lofty groves,
 Behold a Ruin hoary !
The shattered front of Newark's Towers,
 Renowned in Border story.

Fair scenes for childhood's opening bloom,
 For sportive youth to stray in :
For manhood to enjoy his strength :
 And age to wear away in !
Yon cottage seems a bower of bliss,
 A covert for protection
Of tender thoughts, that nestle there—
 The brood of chaste affection.

How sweet, on this autumnal day,
 The wild-wood fruits to gather,
And on my True-love's forehead plant
 A crest of blooming heather !
And what if I enwreathed my own !
 'Twere no offence to reason ;
The sober Hills thus deck their brows
 To meet the wintry season.

I see—but not by sight alone,
 Loved Yarrow, have I won thee ;
A ray of fancy still survives—
 Her sunshine plays upon thee !
Thy ever-youthful waters keep
 A course of lively pleasure :
And gladsome notes my lips can breathe,
 Accordant to the measure.

The vapours linger round the **Heights,**
  They melt, and soon must vanish ;
One hour is theirs, nor more is mine—
  Sad thoughts, which I would banish,
But that **I know, where'er I go,**
  Thy genuine image, Yarrow !
Will dwell with me—to **heighten joy,**
  And cheer my mind in sorrow.

WORDSWORTH.

The River Eden, Cumberland.

EDEN ! till now thy beauty had I viewed
  By glimpses only, and confess with shame
That verse of mine, whate'er its varying mood,
Repeats **but once the sound of thy sweet name :**
Yet fetched from Paradise **that honour came,**
Rightfully borne ; **for Nature gives thee flowers**
That have **no rivals among British bowers;**
And thy bold **rocks are worthy of** their fame.
Measuring thy course, fair **Stream !** at length **I pay**
To my life's neighbour **dues** of neighbourhood :
But I have traced thee on thy winding way
With pleasure sometimes by this thought restrained,—
For things far off we toil, while **many a good**
Not sought, because too near, is never gained.

WORDSWORTH.

To the River Duddon.

SOLE listener, Duddon ! to the breeze that played
  With thy clear voice, I caught the fitful sound
Wafted o'er sullen moss and craggy mound—
Unfruitful solitudes, that seemed to upbraid
The sun in heaven !—but now, to form a shade
For thee, green alders have together wound
Their foliage ; ashes flung their arms around ;
And birch trees risen in silver colonnade.
And thou hast also tempted here to rise,
'Mid sheltering pines, this Cottage rude and grey ;
Whose ruddy children, by the mother's eyes
Carelessly watched, sport through the summer day,
Thy pleased associates :—light as endless May
On infant bosoms lonely Nature lies.

WORDSWORTH.

The Avon.

(*A Feeder of the Annan.*)

AVON—a precious, an immortal name !
  Yet is it one that other rivulets bear
Like this unheard-of, and their channels wear
Like this contented, though unknown to Fame :
For great and sacred is the modest claim
Of Streams to Nature's love, where'er they flow :
And ne'er did Genius slight them, as they go,

Tree, flower, and green herb, feeding without blame.
But Praise can waste her voice on work of tears,
Anguish and death : full oft where innocent blood
Has mixed its current with the limpid **flood**,
Her heaven-offending trophies Glory rears :
Never for like distinction may the good
Shrink from *thy* name, pure Rill, with **unpleased ears**.

WORDSWORTH.

Sonnet.

BROOK ! whose society the Poet seeks,
   Intent his wasted spirits to renew :
And whom the curious Painter doth pursue
Through rocky passes, among flowery creeks,
And tracks thee dancing down thy water-breaks ;
If wish were mine some type of thee to view,
Thee, and not thee thyself, I would not do
Like Grecian Artists, give thee human cheeks,
Channels for tears ; no Naiad shouldst thou be,—
Have neither limbs, feet, feathers, joints, nor hairs
It seems the Eternal Soul is clothed in thee
With purer robes than those of flesh and blood,
And hath bestowed on thee a safer good ;
Unwearied joy, and life without its cares.

WORDSWORTH.

[*From* On Revisiting a Scottish River.]

AND call they this Improvement?—to have changed,
 My native Clyde, thy once romantic shore,
Where Nature's face is banish'd and estranged,
And Heaven reflected in thy wave no more ;
Whose banks, that sweeten'd May-day's breath before,
Lie sere and leafless now in summer's beam,
With sooty exhalations cover'd o'er ;
And for the daisied green-sward, down thy stream,
Unsightly brick-lanes smoke, and clanking engines gleam. . . .

      God has not given
This passion to the heart of man in vain,
For Earth's green face, th' untainted air of Heaven,
And all the bliss of Nature's rustic reign.
For not alone our frame imbibes a stain
From fetid skies ; the spirit's healthy pride,
Fades in their gloom—And therefore I complain,
That thou no more through pastoral scenes shouldst glide,
My Wallace's own stream, and once romantic Clyde !

        THOMAS CAMPBELL.

[*From* Rokeby, Canto i.]

WHERE Orinoco, in his pride,
 Rolls to the main no tribute tide,
But 'gainst broad ocean urges far
A rival sea of roaring war ;

While, in ten thousand eddies driven,
The billows fling their foam to heaven,
And the pale pilot seeks in vain,
Where rolls the river, where the **main**.

SIR WALTER SCOTT.

[*From* Rokeby, Canto ii.]

TEES, full many a fathom low,
  Wears with his rage no common foe;
For pebbly bank, nor sand-bed here,
Nor clay-mound, checks his fierce career,
Condemn'd to mine a channell'd way,
O'er solid sheets of marble grey.

Nor Tees alone, in dawning bright,
Shall **rush** upon **the ravish'd sight;**
But many a tributary stream
Each **from** its own dark dell shall gleam:
Staindrop, who, from her silvan bowers,
Salutes proud Raby's battled towers;
The rural brook of Egliston,
And Balder, named from Odin's son; .
And Greta, to whose banks ere long
We lead the lovers of the song;
And silver Lune, from Stanmore wild,
And fairy Thorsgill's murmuring child,
And last and least, but loveliest still,
Romantic Deepdale's slender rill.

SIR W. SCOTT.

[*From* The Lay of the Last Minstrel, Canto iv.]

SWEET Teviot! on thy silver tide
    The glaring bale-fires blaze no more ;
No longer steel-clad warriors ride
    Along thy wild and willow'd shore ;
Where'er thou wind'st, by dale or hill,
All, all is peaceful, all is still,
    As if thy waves, since Time was born,
Since first they roll'd upon the Tweed,
Had only heard the shepherd's reed,
    Nor started at the bugle-horn.

SIR W. SCOTT.

[*From* Marmion, Introduction to Canto ii.]

RISES the fog-smoke white as snow,
    Thunders the viewless stream below,
Diving, as if condemn'd to lave
Some demon's subterranean cave,
Who, prison'd by enchanter's spell,
Shakes the dark rock with groan and yell.

SIR W. SCOTT.

To the River Otter.

DEAR native brook ! wild streamlet of the West !
   How many various-fated years have passed,
What happy, and what mournful hours, since last
I skimm'd the smooth thin stone along thy breast,
Numbering its light leaps ! Yet so deep imprest
Sink the sweet scenes of childhood, that mine eyes
I never shut amid the sunny ray,
But straight with all their tints thy waters rise,
Thy crossing plank, thy marge with willows gray,
And bedded sand, that vein'd with various dyes,
Gleam'd through thy bright transparence ! On my way,
Visions of childhood ! oft have ye beguiled
Lone manhood's cares, yet waking fondest sighs :
Ah ! that once more I were a careless child !

SAMUEL TAYLOR COLERIDGE.

For a Tablet on the Banks of a Stream.

STRANGER ! awhile upon this mossy bank
   Recline thee. If the Sun rides high, the breeze,
That loves to ripple o er the rivulet,
Will play around thy brow, and the cool sound
Of running waters soothe thee.   Mark how clear
They sparkle o'er the shallows, and behold
Where o'er their surface wheels with restless speed
Yon glossy insect, on the sand below

How its swift shadow flits.   In solitude
The rivulet **is** pure, and trees and herbs,
Bend o'er its salutary course refresh'd,
But passing on amid the haunts of men,
It finds pollution there, and rolls from thence
A tainted stream.   Seek'st thou for HAPPINESS ?
Go, Stranger, sojourn in the woodland cot
Of INNOCENCE, and thou shalt find her there.

ROBERT SOUTHEY.

[*From* The Ebb Tide.]

SLOWLY thy flowing tide
    Came in, old Avon ! scarcely did mine eyes,
As watchfully I roam'd thy green-wood side,
    Perceive its gentle rise.

With many a stroke and strong
The labouring boatmen upward plied their oars,
Yet little way they made, though labouring long
    Between thy winding shores.

Now down thine ebbing tide
The unlabour'd boat falls rapidly along ;
The solitary helm's-man sits to guide,
    And sings an idle song.

Now o'er the rocks that lay
So silent late, the shallow current roars ;
Fast flow thy waters on their seaward way
    Through wider-spreading shores.

OUTHEY.

[*From* Thalaba the Destroyer, Book vii.]

SILENT and calm the river roll'd along,
And at the verge arrived
Of that fair garden, o'er a rocky bed
Toward the mountain-base,
Still full and silent held its even way.
But farther as they went its deepening sound
Louder and louder in the distance rose,
As if it forced its stream
Struggling through crags along a narrow pass.
And lo ! where raving o'er a hollow course
The ever-flowing flood
Foams in a thousand whirlpools ! There adown
The perforated rock
Plunge the whole waters ; so precipitous,
So fathomless a fall,
That their earth-shaking roar came deaden'd up
Like subterranean thunders.

SOUTHEY.

[*From* Roderick, the Last of the Goths.]

Covadonga.

A MOUNTAIN rivulet,
Now calm and lovely in its summer course,
Held by those huts its everlasting way
Towards Pionia.   They whose flocks and herds

Drink of its water call it Deva. Here
Pelayo southward up the ruder vale
Traced it, his guide unerring. Amid heaps
Of mountain wreck, on either side thrown high,
The wide-spread traces of its wintry might,
The tortuous channel wound ; o'er beds of sand
Here silently it flows ; here from the rock
Rebutted, curls and eddies ; plunges here
Precipitate ; here roaring among crags,
It leaps and foams and whirls and hurries on.

SOUTHEY.

[*From* Madoc in Wales.]

Lincoya.

A T length we came
  Where the great river, amid shoals and banks
And islands, growth of its own gathering spoils,
Through many a branching channel, wide and full,
Rush'd to the main. The gale was strong ; and safe,
Amid the uproar of conflicting tides,
Our gallant vessels rode. A stream as broad
And turbid, when it leaves the Land of Hills,
Old Severn rolls ; but banks so fair as these
Old Severn views not in his Land of Hills,
Nor even where his turbid waters swell
And sully the salt sea.

SOUTHEY.

[*From* The Poet's Pilgrimage to Waterloo.]

The **Sacred** Mountain.

A GENTLE river wound **its quiet way**
  Through this sequester'd glade, **meandering wide ;**
Smooth as a mirror here **the surface lay,**
  Where the pure lotus, floating **in its pride,**
Enjoy'd the breath **of heaven, the sun's warm beam,**
And the cool freshness of its **native stream.**

Here o'er green weeds whose tresses waved **outspread,**
  With silent lapse the glassy waters **run ;**
Here in fleet motion o'er a pebbly bed
  Gliding they glance and ripple to the sun ;
The stirring breeze that swept them in its flight,
Raised on the stream **a** shower of sparkling light.

SOUTHEY.

[*From* Lines written in an Album.]

The **Rotha.**

L OVELIER river is there none
  Underneath an English sun ;
From its source it issues bright,
Upon hoar Helvellyn's height,
Flowing where its summer voice
Makes the mountain herds rejoice ;
Down the dale it issues then,
Not polluted there by **men ;**

While its lucid waters take
Their pastoral course from lake to lake,
Please the eye in every part,
Lull the ear, and soothe the heart,
Till into Windermere sedate
They flow and uncontaminate.

SOUTHEY.

[*From* The Village Patriarch, Book v.]

FIVE rivers, like the fingers of a hand,
 Flung from black mountains, mingle, and are one
Where sweetest valleys quit the wild and grand,
And eldest forests, o'er the silvan Don,
Bid their immortal brother journey on,
A stately pilgrim, watch'd by all the hills.
Say, shall we wander where, through warriors' graves,
The infant Yewden, mountain-cradled, trills
Her Doric notes?   Or, where the Locksley raves
Of broil and battle, and the rocks and caves
Dream yet of ancient days?   Or, where the sky
Darkens o'er Rivilin, the clear and cold,
That throws his blue length, like a snake, from high?
Or, where deep azure brightens into gold
O'er Sheaf, that mourns in Eden?   Or, where roll'd
On tawny sands, through regions passion-wild,
And groves of love, in jealous beauty dark,
Complains the Porter, Nature's thwarted child,

Born in the waste, like headlong Wiming? Hark !
The poised hawk calls thee, Village Patriarch !
He calls thee to his mountains! Up, away !
Up, up, to Stanedge ! higher still ascend,
Till kindred rivers, from the summit grey,
To distant seas their course in beauty bend,
And, like the lives of human millions, blend
Disparted waves in one immensity !

EBENEZER ELLIOTT.

The Nile.

IT flows through old hush'd Ægypt and its sands,
   Like some grave mighty thought threading a dream,
 And times and things, as in that vision, seem
Keeping along it their eternal stands,—
Caves, pillars, pyramids, the shepherd bands
   That roamed through the young world, the glory extreme
   Of high Sesostris, and that southern beam,
The laughing queen that caught the world's great hands.

Then comes a mightier silence, stern and strong,
As of a world left empty of its throng,
   And the void weighs on us ; and then we wake,
And hear the fruitful stream lapsing along
   'Twixt villages, and think how we shall take
   Our own calm journey on for human sake.

LEIGH HUNT.

[*From* The Rivulet.]

THIS little rill, that from the springs
    Of yonder grove its current brings,
Plays on the slope awhile, and then
Goes prattling into groves again,
Oft to its warbling waters drew
My little feet when life was new. . . .

And when the days of boyhood came,
And I had grown in love with fame,
Duly I sought thy banks, and tried
My first rude numbers by thy side. . . .
Thou, ever-joyous rivulet,
Dost dimple, leap, and prattle yet ;
And sporting with the sands that pave
The windings of thy silver wave,
And dancing to thy own wild chime,
Thou laughest at the lapse of time.
The same sweet sounds are in my ear
My early childhood loved to hear ;
As pure thy limpid waters run ;
As bright they sparkle to the sun ;
As fresh and thick the bending ranks
Of herbs that line thy oozy banks ;
The violet there, in soft May dew,
Comes up, as modest and as blue ;
As green amid thy current's stress,
Floats the scarce-rooted watercress :

River Rhyme.

And the brown ground-bird, **in thy glen,**
Still chirps as merrily as then.

Yet a few years shall pass away,
And I, all trembling, weak, and gray,
Bowed to the earth, which waits to **fold**
My ashes in the embracing mould,
(If haply the **dark** will of Fate
Indulge my life **so long a date),**
May **come for the last time to look**
Upon my childhood's **favourite brook.**
Then dimly on my eye shall gleam
The sparkle of thy dancing stream ;
And faintly on my ear shall fall
Thy prattling current's merry call ;
Yet shalt thou flow as glad and bright
As when thou met'st my infant sight.

And I shall sleep—and on thy side,
As ages after ages glide,
Children their early sports shall try,
And pass to hoary age and die.
But thou, unchanged from year **to year,**
Gaily shalt play and glitter here ;
Amid young flowers and tender **grass**
Thy endless infancy shall pass ;
And, singing down thy narrow glen,
Shalt mock the fading race of men.

WILLIAM CULLEN BRYANT.

[*From* Green River.]

WHEN breezes are soft and skies are fair,
    I steal an hour from study and care,
And hie me away to the woodland scene,
Where wanders the stream with waters of green,
As if the bright fringe of herbs on its brink
Had given their stain to the wave they drink;
And they, whose meadows it murmurs through,
Have named the stream from its own fair hue.

Yet pure its waters—its shallows are bright
With coloured pebbles and sparkles of light,
And clear the depths where its eddies play,
And dimples deepen and whirl away;
And the plane-tree's speckled arms o'ershot
The swifter current that mines its root,
Through whose shifting leaves, as you walk the hill,
The quivering glimmer of sun and rill
With a sudden flash on the eye is thrown,
Like the ray that streams from the diamond-stone.
.   .   .   .

Yet fair as thou art, thou shunnest to glide,
Beautiful stream! by the village side;
But windest away from haunts of men,
To quiet valley and shaded glen;
And forest, and meadow, and slope of hill,
Around thee, are lonely, lovely, and still,
Lonely—save when, by thy rippling tides,
From thicket to thicket the angler glides;

Or the simpler comes, with basket and book,
For herbs of power on thy banks to look ;
Or haply, some idle dreamer, like me,
To wander, and muse, and gaze on **thee,**
Still—save the chief of birds that feed
On the river cherry and **seedy reed,**
And thy **own** wild music gushing **out**
With mellow murmur of fairy **shout,**
From dawn to the blush of another day,
Like traveller singing along his way.

That fairy music I never hear,
Nor gaze on **those waters** so green **and clear,**
And mark them winding away **from sight,**
Darkened with shade or flashing with **light,**
While o'er them the vine to its **thicket clings,**
And the zephyr stoops to **freshen his wings,**
But I wish that fate had left me free,
To wander those quiet **haunts** with thee.

W. C. BRYANT.

[*From* Clyde.]

BOAST not, great Forth, thy broad majestic tide,
    Beyond the graceful modesty of Clyde ;
Though famed Mæander, in the poet's dream,
Ne'er led **through** fairer fields, his wandering stream.
Bright wind thy mazy links on Stirling's plain,
Which, oft departing, still return again ;

And wheeling round and round in sportive mood,
The nether stream turns back to meet the upper flood.
Now sunk in shades, now bright in open day,
Bright Clyde, in simple beauty, winds his way.

JOHN WILSON.

[*From* Childe Harold's Pilgrimage, Canto i.]

DARK Guadiana rolls his power along
　　In sullen billows, murmuring and vast,

GEORGE, LORD BYRON.

[*From* Childe Harold's Pilgrimage, Canto iii.]

ADIEU to thee, fair Rhine! How long delighted
　　The stranger fain would linger on his way!
Thine is a scene alike where souls united
Or lonely Contemplation thus might stray;
And could the ceaseless vultures cease to prey
On self-condemning bosoms, it were here,
Where Nature, nor too sombre nor too gay,
Wild, but not rude, awful, yet not austere,
Is to the mellow Earth as Autumn to the year.

Adieu to thee again! a vain adieu!
There can be no farewell to scene like thine;
The mind is colour'd by thy every hue;
And if reluctantly the eyes resign
Their cherish'd gaze upon thee, lovely Rhine!

'Tis with the thankful heart of parting praise ;
More mighty spots may rise, more glaring shine,
But none unite in one attaching maze
The brilliant, fair, and soft,—the glories of old **days.**

Byron.

[*From* Childe Harold's Pilgrimage, Canto iii.]

B^{UT} Thou, exulting and abounding river !
   Making thy waves a blessing as they flow
Through banks whose beauty would endure for ever,
Could man but leave thy bright creation **so,**
Nor its fair promise from the surface mow
With the sharp scythe of conflict,—then to see
Thy valley of sweet waters, **were to** know,
Earth paved like Heaven ; and to seem such to me,
Even now what wants thy stream ?—that it should Lethe be.

Byron.

[*From* Childe Harold's Pilgrimage, Canto iv.]

T^{HE} roar of waters !—from **the** headlong height
   Velino cleaves the **wave-worn** precipice ;
The fall of waters ! rapid as the light
The flashing mass foams shaking the abyss ;
The hell of waters ! where they howl and hiss,
And boil in endless torture ; while the sweat
Of their great agony, wrung out from this
Their Phlegethon, curls round the rocks of jet
That guard the gulf around, in pitiless horror **set,**

P

And mounts in spray the skies, and thence again
Returns in an increasing shower, which round,
With its unemptied cloud of gentle rain,
Is an eternal April to the ground,
Making it all one emerald :—how profound
The gulf ! and how the giant element
From rock to rock leaps with delirious bound,
Crushing the cliffs, which, downward worn and rent
With his fierce footsteps, yield in chasms a fearful vent !

To the broad column which rolls on, and shows
More like the fountain of an infant sea
Torn from the womb of mountains by the throes
Of a new world, than only thus to be
Parent of rivers, which flow gushingly,
With many windings, through the vale :—Look back !
Lo, where it comes like an eternity,
As if to sweep down all things in its track,
Charming the eye with dread,—a matchless cataract.

BYRON.

[*From* Stanzas to the Po.]

RIVER, that rollest by the ancient walls,
 Where dwells the lady of my love, when she
Walks by thy brink, and there perchance recalls
 A faint and fleeting memory of me ;

What if thy deep and ample stream should be
 A mirror of my heart, where she may read

The thousand thoughts I now betray to thee,
  Wild as thy wave, and headlong as thy speed !

What do I say-—a mirror of my heart?
  Are not thy waters sweeping, dark, and strong?
Such as my feelings were and are, thou art ;
  And such as thou art were my passions long.

Time may have somewhat tamed them,—not for ever ;
  Thou overflow'st thy banks, and not for aye
Thy bosom overboils, congenial river !
  Thy floods subside, and mine have sunk away :

But left long wrecks behind, and now again,
  Borne on our old unchanged career, we move :
Thou tendest wildly onwards to the main,
  And I—to loving *one* I should not love.

BYRON.

The Shannon.

RIVER of billows, to whose mighty heart
  The tide-wave rushes of the Atlantic sea ;
River of quiet depths, by cultured lea,
Romantic wood, or city's crowded mart ;
River of old poetic founts, which start
From their lone mountain-cradles, wild and free,
Nursed with the fawns, lulled by the wood-lark's glee,
And cushat's hymeneal song apart :
River of chieftains, whose baronial halls,

Like veteran warders, watch each wave-worn steep,
Portumna's towers, Bunratty's royal walls,
    Carrick's stern rock, the Geraldine's gray keep—
River of dark mementoes ! must I close
My lips with Limerick's wrong, with Aughrim's woes?

SIR AUBREY DE VERE.

The Rhine.

WE'VE sailed through banks of green,
    Where the wild waves fret and quiver,
And we've down the Danube been,
    The dark, deep, thundering river !
We've threaded the Elbe and Rhone,
    The Tiber and blood-dyed Seine,
And have watched where the blue Garonne
    Goes laughing to meet the main :
        But what is so lovely, what is so grand,
        As the river that runs through Rhine-land?

On the Rhine river were we born,
    Midst its flowers and famous wines,
And we know that our country's morn
    With a treble-sweet aspect shines.
Let other lands boast their flowers,
    Let other men dream wild dreams,
Let them hope they've a land like ours,
    And a stream like our stream of streams :
        Yet what is half so bright or so grand
        As the river that runs through Rhine-land?

Are we smit by the blinding sun
  That fell on our tender youth?
Do we, coward-like, shrink and shun
  The thought-telling touch of Truth?
On our heads be the sin, then, set!
  We'll bear all the shame divine:
But we'll never disown the debt
  That we owe to our noble Rhine!
    O, the Rhine! the Rhine! the broad and the grand,
    Is the river that runs through Rhine-land!

BRYAN WALLER PROCTER.

For a Streamlet.

TRAVELLER, note! Although I seem
  But a little sparkling stream,
I come from regions where the sun
Dwelleth when his toil is done;
From yon proud hills in the West,
Thence I come, and never rest,
Till (curling round the mountain's feet)
I find myself 'mid pastures sweet,
Vernal, green, and ever gay;
And then I gently slide away,
A thing of silence,—till I cast
My life into the sea at last!

B. W. PROCTER.

Arethusa.

ARETHUSA arose
 From her couch of snows
In the Acroceraunian mountains,—
 From cloud and from crag,
 With many a jag,
Shepherding her bright fountains.
 She leapt down the rocks,
 With her rainbow locks
Streaming among the streams ;—
 Her steps paved with green
 The downward ravine
Which slopes to the western gleams :
 And gliding and springing
 She went, ever singing,
In murmurs as soft as sleep ;
 The Earth seemed to love her,
 And Heaven smiled above her,
As she lingered towards the deep.

 Then Alpheus bold
 On his glacier cold
With his trident the mountains strook ;
 And opened a chasm
 In the rocks ;—with the spasm
All Erymanthus shook.
 And the black south wind
 It concealed behind

The urns of the silent snow,
  The earthquake and thunder
  Did rend in sunder
The bars of the springs below.
  The beard and the hair
  Of the River-god were
Seen through the torrent's **sweep,**
  As he followed the light
  Of the fleet Nymph's flight
To the brink **of the Dorian deep.**

  "Oh, save me! Oh, guide me!
  And bid the deep hide me,
For he grasps me now by the hair!"
  The loud Ocean heard
  To its blue depth stirred,
And divided at her prayer;
  And under the water
  The Earth's white daughter
Fled like a sunny **beam;**
  Behind her descended
  Her billows, unblended
With the brackish Dorian stream.
  Like a gloomy stain
  On the emerald main,
Alpheus rushed behind,—
  As an eagle pursuing
  A dove to its ruin,
Down the stream of the cloudy wind.

Under the bowers,
  Where the Ocean Powers
Sit on their pearlèd thrones ;
  Through the coral woods
  Of the weltering floods ;
Over heaps of unvalued stones ;
  Through the dim beams
  Which amid the streams
Weave a network of coloured light ;
  And under the caves,
  Where the shadowy waves
Are as green as the forest's night :—
  Outspeeding the shark,
  And the sword-fish dark,
Under the ocean foam,
  And up through the rifts
  Of the mountain clifts,—
They past to their Dorian home.

  And now from their fountains
  In Enna's mountains,
Down one vale where the morning basks,
  Like friends once parted
  Groan single-hearted,
They ply their watery tasks.
  At sunrise they leap
  From their cradles steep
In the cave of the shelving hill ;
  At noon-tide they flow
  Through the woods below,

And the meadows of Asphodel ;
   And at night they sleep
   In the rocking deep
Beneath the Ortygian shore,—
   Like spirits that lie
   In the azure sky,
When they love but live no more.

PERCY BYSSHE SHELLEY.

[*From* Alastor.]

THE rivulet,
   Wanton and wild, through many a green ravine
Beneath the forest flowed.   Sometimes it fell
Among the moss with hollow harmony,
Dark and profound.   Now on the polished stones
It danced ; like childhood, laughing as it went :
Then, through the plain in tranquil wanderings crept,
Reflecting every herb and drooping bud
That overhung its quietness.—"O stream !
Whose source is inaccessibly profound,
Whither do thy mysterious waters tend ?
Thou imagest my life.   Thy darksome stillness,
Thy dazzling waves, thy low and hollow gulphs,
Thy searchless fountain, and invisible course
Have each their type in me : and the wide sky
And measureless ocean may declare as soon
What oozy cavern or what wandering cloud
Contains thy waters, as the universe

Tell where these living thoughts reside, when stretched
Upon thy flowers my bloodless limbs shall waste
I' the passing wind !"

SHELLEY.

[*From* Evening, Ponte-a-Mare, Pisa.]

AND evening's breath, wandering here and there
  Over the quivering surface of the stream,
Wakes not one ripple from its summer dream.

SHELLEY.

The River Clwyd in North Wales.

O CAMBRIAN river ! with slow music gliding
  By pastoral hills, old woods, and ruin'd towers ;
Now midst thy reeds and golden willows hiding,
Now gleaming forth by some rich bank of flowers ;
Long flow'd the current of my life's clear hours
Onward with them, whose voice yet haunts my dream,
Tho' time and change, and other mightier powers,
Far from thy side have borne me.   Thou, smooth stream
Art winding still thy sunny meads along,
Murmuring to cottage and gray hall thy song,
Low, sweet, unchanged.   *My* being's tide hath pass'd
Through rocks and storms ; yet will I not complain,
If, thus wrought free and pure from earthly stain,
Brightly its waves may reach their parent deep at last.

FELICIA DOROTHEA HEMANS.

To the Nile.

SON of the **old** moon-mountains African !
   Stream of the Pyramid **and Crocodile** !
We call thee fruitful, and **that very while**
A desert fills our seeing's inward **span** :
Nurse of swart nations **since the world began,**
Art thou so fruitful ? **or dost** thou **beguile**
Those men to honour thee, who, **worn with toil,**
Rest them a space 'twixt Cairo and Deccan ?
O may dark fancies err ! They surely **do ;**
'Tis **ignorance that makes a barren waste**
Of all beyond itself. Thou dost bedew
Green rushes like our rivers, and dost taste
The pleasant sun-rise. Green isles hast thou **too,**
And to the **sea as happily dost haste.**
JOHN KEATS.

[*From* Stanzas.]

IN a drear-nighted December,
   Too happy, happy brook,
Thy bubblings ne'er remember
Apollo's summer look ;
But with a sweet forgetting,
They stay their crystal fretting,
Never, never petting
About the frozen time.
KEATS.

[*From* Endymion. Book i.]

THIS river does not see the naked sky,
   Till it begins to progress silverly
Around the western border of the wood,
Whence, from a certain spot, its winding flood
Seems at the distance like a crescent moon.

KEATS.

[*From* Endymion, Book i.]

A RIVER, clear, brimful, and flush
   With crystal mocking of the trees and sky.

KEATS.

[*From* Endymion, Book i.]

A BROOK,—whose silver ramble
   Down twenty little falls through reeds and bramble,
Tracing along, it brought me to a cave,
Whence it ran brightly forth, and white did lave
The nether sides of mossy stones and rock,—
'Mong which it gurgled blithe adieus, to mock
Its own sweet grief at parting.

KEATS.

[*From* What I have Heard.]

YET every little brook is known,
By a voice that is **its own,**
Each exulting in the glee,
Of its new prosperity.

HARTLEY COLERIDGE.

[*From* What I have Heard.]

I'VE **heard** the many-sounding **seas,**
And all their various harmonies :—
The tumbling tempest's dismal roar,
On the waste and wreck-strew'd shore—
The howl and the wail **of the prison'd waves,**
Clamouring in the ancient caves,
Like a stifled pain that asks for pity :—
And I have heard the sea at **peace,**
When all its fearful noises **cease,**
Lost in one soft and multitudinous ditty,
Most like the murmur **of a** far off city :—
Nor less the blither notes I **know,**
To which the inland waters flow ;—
The rush of rocky-bedded rivers,
That madly dash themselves to shivers ;
But anon, more prudent growing,
O'er countless pebbles smoothly flowing,

With a dull continuous roar,
Hie they onward, evermore :
To their everlasting tune,
When the sun is high at noon,
The little billows, quick and quicker,
Weave their mazes, thick and thicker,
And beneath in dazzling glances,
Labyrinthine lightning dances,
Snaky network intertwining,
With thousand molten colours shining :
Mosaic rich with living light,
With rainbow jewels gaily dight—
Such pavement never, well I ween,
Was made, by monarch or magician,
For Arab, or Egyptian queen ;
'Tis gorgeous as a prophet's vision ;
And I ken the brook, how sweet it tinkles,
As 'cross the moon-light green it twinkles,
Or heard, not seen, 'mid tangled wood,
Where the soft stock-dove lulls her brood,
With her one note of all most dear—
More soothing to the heart than ear.

H. COLERIDGE.

[*From* From Petrarch.]

AND deep and low, the lucid rill, that weaves
 Its murmuring mazes in the flowery leas,
Warbled along its old monotonies.

H. COLERIDGE.

Niagara.

FLOW on forever, in thy glorious robe
    Of terror and of beauty.   Yea, flow **on**
Unfathomed and resistless.   **God** hath set
His rainbow on thy **forehead; and the cloud**
Mantled around thy feet.   And he doth give
Thy voice of thunder **power to** speak of Him
Eternally,—bidding the lip of man
Keep silence,—and upon thy rocky altar pour
Incense of awe-struck praise.

                Ah ! who **can dare**
To lift the insect trump of earthly **hope,**
Or love, or sorrow, 'mid the peal sublime
Of thy tremendous hymn? Even **ocean shrinks**
Back from thy brotherhood, and **all his waves**
Retire abashed.   **For he doth sometimes seem**
To sleep like a spent laborer, and recall
His wearied billows from their vexing play,
And lull them to a cradle-calm ; but thou,
With everlasting, undecaying tide
Dost rest not, night or **day.**   The morning stars,
When first they sang o'er young creation's birth,
Heard thy deep anthem ; **and** those wrecking fires,
That wait the archangel's signal to dissolve
The solid earth, shall find Jehovah's name
Graven, as with a thousand diamond spears,
On thine unending volume.

                    Every leaf,
That lifts itself within thy wide domain,
Doth gather greenness from thy living spray,
Yet tremble at the baptism.   Lo !—yon birds
Do boldly venture near, and bathe their wing
Amid thy mist and foam.   'Tis meet for them
To touch thy garment's hem, and lightly stir
The snowy leaflets of thy vapor-wreath,
For they may sport unharmed amid the cloud,
Or listen at the echoing gate of heaven
Without reproof.   But as for us, it seems
Scarce lawful, with our broken tones, to speak
Familiarly of thee.   Methinks, to tint
Thy glorious features with our pencil's point,
Or woo thee to the tablet of a song,
Were profanation.

                    Thou dost make the soul
A wondering witness of thy majesty ;
But as it presses with delirious joy
To pierce thy vestibule, dost chain its step,
And tame its rapture with the humbling view
Of its own nothingness, bidding it stand
In the dread presence of the Invisible,
As if to answer to its God through thee.
                              LYDIA H. SIGOURNEY.

[*From* The River.]

INFANT of the weeping hills,
   Nursling of the springs and rills,
Growing River, flowing ever,
Wimpling, dimpling, staying never,—
Lisping, gurgling, ever going,
Lipping, slipping, ever flowing,
Toying round the polished stone,
Kiss the sedge and journey on.
Here's a creek where bubbles come,
Whirling make your ball of foam.
There's a nook so deep and cool,
Sleep into a glassy pool.
Breaking, gushing,
Downward rushing,
Narrowing green against the bank,
Where the alders grow in rank,--
Thence recoiling,
Outward boiling,
Fret, in rough shingly shallows wide,
Your difficult way to yonder side.
Thence away, aye away,
Bickering down the sunny day,
In the Sea, in yonder West,
Lose yourself, and be at rest.
Thus from darkness weeping out,
Flows our infant Life away,

Murmuring now the checks about,
Singing now in onward play;
Deepening, whirling,
Darkly swirling,
Downward sucked in eddying coves;
Boiling with tumultuous loves;
Widening o'er the worldly sands;
Kissing full the cultured lands;
Dim with trouble, glory-lit,
Heaven still bending over it;
Changing still, yet ever going,
Onward, downward, ever flowing.

THOMAS AIRD.

[*From* Phantasmion, Part iii., Chap. iv.]

Zelneth's Song.

I WAS a brook in straitest channel pent,
    Forcing 'mid rocks and stones my toilsome way,
A scanty brook in wandering well nigh spent;
But now with thee, rich stream, conjoin'd I stray,
Through golden meads the river sweeps along,
Murmuring its deep full joy in gentlest undersong.

I crept through desert moor and gloomy shade,
My waters ever vex'd, yet sad and slow,
My waters ever steep'd in baleful shade:
But whilst with thee, rich stream, conjoin'd I flow,
E'en in swift course the river seems to rest,
Blue sky, bright bloom, and verdure imag'd on its breast.

And, whilst with thee I roam through regions bright,
Beneath kind love's serene and gladsome sky,
A thousand happy things that seek the light,
Till now in darkest shadow forc'd to lie,
Up through the illumin'd waters nimbly run,
To show their forms and hues in the all-revealing sun.

SARA COLERIDGE.

[*From* Phantasmion, Part iii., Chap. iii.]

SLOW rills that wind like snakes amid the grass.

S. COLERIDGE.

Two Rivers.

THY summer voice, Musketaquit,
    Repeats the music of the rain ;
But sweeter rivers pulsing flit
Through thee, as thou through Concord Plain.

Thou in thy narrow banks are pent :
The stream I love unbounded goes
Through flood and sea and firmament ;
Through light, through life, it forward flows.

I see the inundation sweet,
I hear the spending of the stream
Through years, through men, through nature fleet,
Through love and thought, through power and dream.

Musketaquit, a goblin strong,
Of shard and flint makes jewels gay ;
They lose their grief who hear his song,
And where he winds is the day of day.

So forth and brighter fares my stream,—
Who drink it shall not thirst again ;
No darkness stains its equal gleam,
And ages drop in it like rain.

RALPH WALDO EMERSON.

[*From* Woodnotes.—ii.]

THE river knows the way to the sea ;
 Without a pilot it runs and falls,
Blessing all lands with its charity.

EMERSON.

[*From* Roland's Tower.]

LIKE a courser starting from the spur,
 Rushes the deep-blue current of the Rhine.

LETITIA ELIZABETH LANDON.

[*From* King Arthur, Book i.]

AND the still river shining as it flows,
 Calm as a soul on which the heavens repose.

EDWARD, LORD LYTTON.

[*From* Kenelm Chillingley, Book iii., Chap. xi.]

Love's Quarrel.

STANDING by the river, gazing on the river,
  See it paved with starbeams; heaven is at our feet.
Now the wave is troubled, now the rushes quiver;
  Vanished is the starlight—it was a deceit.

Comes a little cloudlet 'twixt ourselves and heaven,
  And from all the river fades the silver track;
Put thine arms around me, whisper low " Forgiven !"—
  See how on the river starlight settles back.

LORD LYTTON.

[*From* The Dispute of the Poets.]

A SHADOWY rill
  Melodious with the chime of falls as sweet
As (heard by Pan in Arethusan glades)
The silvery talk of meeting Naïades.

LORD LYTTON.

[*From* The Poet to the Dead.]

GLIDES the brooklet thro' the rushes,
  Now with dipping boughs at play,
Now with quicker music-gushes
  Where the pebbles chafe the way.

LORD LYTTON.

[*From* To the River Charles.]

RIVER ! that in silence windest
   Through the meadows, bright and free,
Till at length thy rest thou findest
   In the bosom of the sea !

Four long years of mingled feeling,
   Half in rest, and half in strife,
I have seen thy waters stealing
   Onward, like the stream of life.

Thou hast taught me, Silent River !
   Many a lesson, deep and long ;
Thou hast been a generous giver ;
   I can give thee but a song.

Oft in sadness and in illness
   I have watched thy current glide,
Till the beauty of its stillness
   Overflowed me like a tide.

And in better hours and brighter,
   When I saw thy waters gleam,
I have felt my heart beat lighter,
   And leap onward with thy stream.

          HENRY WADSWORTH LONGFELLOW.

[*From* The Bridge.]

I STOOD on the bridge at midnight,
  As the clocks were striking the hour,
And the moon rose o'er **the city,**
  Behind the dark church tower.

I saw her bright reflection
  In the waters under me,
Like a golden goblet falling
  And sinking into the sea.

And far in the hazy distance
  Of that lovely night in June,
The blaze of the flaming furnace
  Gleamed redder than the **moon.**

Among the long, black **rafters**
  The wavering shadows lay,
And the current that came from the **ocean**
  Seemed to lift and bear them away ;

As, sweeping and eddying through them,
  Rose the belated tide,
And, streaming into the moonlight,
  The sea-weed floated wide.

And like those waters rushing
  Among the wooden piers,

A flood of thoughts came o'er me
    That filled my eyes with tears.

How often, O, how often,
    In the days that had gone by,
I had stood on that bridge at midnight
    And gazed on that wave and sky !

How often, O, how often,
    I had wished that the ebbing tide
Would bear me away on its bosom
    O'er the ocean wild and wide !

For my heart was hot and restless,
    And my life was full of care,
And the burden laid upon me
    Seemed greater than I could bear.

But now it has fallen from me,
    It is buried in the sea ;
And only the sorrow of others
    Throws its shadow over me.

Yet whenever I cross the river
    On its bridge with wooden piers,
Like the odour of brine from the ocean
    Comes the thought of other years.

LONGFELLOW.

[*From* The Mad River, in the White Mountains.]

Traveller.

WHY dost thou wildly rush and **roar,**
    Mad River, O Mad River?
Wilt thou **not pause and cease to pour**
Thy hurrying, headlong waters o'er
    This rocky shelf forever?

What secret trouble stirs **thy breast?**
    Why all this fret and flurry?
Dost thou not know that what is **best**
In this too restless world **is rest**
    From over-work **and worry?**

  .   .   .   .

The River.

A brooklet nameless and unknown
    Was I at first, resembling
A little child, that all alone
Comes venturing down the stairs of **stone,**
    Irresolute and trembling.

Later, by wayward fancies led,
    For the wide world I panted;
Out of the forest dark and dread
Across the open fields I fled,
    Like one pursued and haunted.

I tossed my arms, I sang aloud,
  My voice exultant blending
With thunder from the passing cloud,
The wind, the forest bent and bowed,
  The rush of rain descending.

I heard the distant ocean call,
  Imploring and entreating ;
Drawn onward, o'er this rocky wall
I plunged, and the loud waterfall
  Made answer to the greeting.

And now, beset with many ills,
  A toilsome life I follow ;
Compelled to carry from the hills
These logs to the impatient mills
  Below there in the hollow.

Yet something ever cheers and charms
  The rudeness of my labours ;
Daily I water with these arms
The cattle of a hundred farms,
  And have the birds for neighbours.

Men call me mad, and well they may,
  When, full of rage and trouble,
I burst my banks of sand and clay,
And sweep their wooden bridge away,
  Like withered reeds or stubble.

Now go and **write** thy little rhyme,
    As of thine own creating.
Thou seest the day is past its prime ;
I can no longer waste my time ;
    The mills are tired of waiting.

LONGFELLOW.

[*From* Evangeline, Introduction.]

RIVERS that water the woodlands,
    Darkened by shadows of earth, but reflecting an
    image of heaven.

LONGFELLOW.

[*From* Evangeline, Part ii.]

TO the south, ...
    Fretted with sands and rocks, and swept by the wind
    of the desert,
Numberless torrents, with ceaseless sound, descend to the
    ocean,
Like the great chords of **a harp, in** loud and **solemn**
    vibrations.

LONGFELLOW.

[*From* Hermes Trismegistus.]

STILL through Egypt's desert places
    Flows the lordly Nile ;
From its banks the great stone faces
    Gaze with patient smile.

LONGFELLOW.

[*From* Sounds.]

HEARKEN, hearken !
    The rapid river carrieth
Many noises underneath
    The hoary ocean :
Teaching his solemnity
Sounds of inland life and glee
Learnt beside the waving tree
When the winds in summer prank
Toss the shades from bank to bank,
And the quick rains, in emotion
Which rather gladdens earth than grieves,
Count and visibly rehearse
The pulses of the universe
Upon the summer leaves—
Learnt among the lilies straight,
When they bow them to the weight
Of many bees whose hidden hum
Seemeth from themselves to come—

Learnt among the grasses green
Where the rustling mice are seen
By the gleaming, as they run,
Of their quick eyes in the sun. . . .
All these sounds the river telleth,
Softened to an undertone,
Which ever and anon he swelleth
By a burden of his own,
    In the ocean's ear :
Ay, and ocean seems to hear
With an inward gentle scorn,
Smiling to his caverns worn.
ELIZABETH BARRETT BROWNING.

[*From* Aurora Leigh, Book i.]

H EADLONG leaps
    Of waters, that cry out for joy or fear
In leaping through the palpitating pines,
Like a white soul tossed out to eternity
With thrills of time upon it.
E. B. BROWNING.

[*From* Aurora Leigh, Book vii.]

B UT presently the winding Rhone
    Washed out the moonlight large along his banks,
Which strained their yielding curves out clear and clean
To hold it,—shadow of town and castle blurred
Upon the hurrying river.
E. B. BROWNING.

[*From* Aurora Leigh, Book vii.]

THE river trailing like a silver cord
 Through all, and curling loosely, both before
And after, over the whole stretch of land.

E. B. BROWNING.

[*From* An Island.]

AND brooks, that glass in different strengths
 All colours in disorder,
Or, gathering up their silver lengths
 Beside their winding border,
Sleep, haunted through the slumber hidden,
By lilies white as dreams in Eden.

E. B. BROWNING.

[*From* The Spring and the Brook.]

BUT Thou, O lively Brook ! whose fruitful way
 Brings with it mirror'd smiles, and green, and
  flowers,—
Child of all scenes, companion of all hours,
Taking the simple cheer of every day.

LORD HOUGHTON.

[*From* The Water Babies, Chap. i.]

The River's Song.

CLEAR and cool, clear and cool,
　　By laughing shallow, and dreaming pool ;
Cool and clear, cool and clear,
　　By shining shingle, and foaming weir ;
　　　Under the crag where the ouzel sings,
　　　And the ivied wall where the church bell rings,
Undefiled, for the undefiled ;
　　Play by me, bathe in me, mother and child.

　　　Dank and foul, dank and foul,
　　By the smoky town in its murky cowl ;
　　　Foul and dank, foul and dank,
　　By wharf and sewer and slimy bank ;
Darker and darker the further I go,
Baser and baser the richer I grow ;
　　Who dare sport with the sin defiled ?
　　Shrink from me, turn from me, mother and child.

　　　Strong and free, strong and free,
　　The flood-gates are open, away to the sea,
　　　Free and strong, free and strong,
　　Cleansing my streams as I hurry along,
To the golden sands, and the leaping bar,
And the taintless tide that awaits me afar,

As I lose myself in the infinite main,
Like a soul that has sinned and is pardoned again.
Undefiled, for the undefiled,
Play by me, bathe in me, mother and child.

      CHARLES KINGSLEY.

A River Pool.

SWEET streamlet basin ! at thy side
 Weary and faint within me cried
My longing heart,—In such pure deep
How sweet it were to sit and sleep ;
To feel each passage from without
Close up,—above me and about,
Those circling waters crystal clear,
That calm, impervious atmosphere !
There on thy pearly pavement pure
To lean, and feel myself secure,
Or through the dim-lit inter-space,
Afar at whiles up-gazing trace
The dimpling bubbles dance around
Upon thy smooth exterior face ;
Or idly list the dreamy sound
Of ripples lightly flung, above
That home of peace, if not of love.

      ARTHUR HUGH CLOUGH.

[*From* Elegiacs.—i.]

FROM thy far sources, 'mid mountains airily climbing,
  Pass to the rich lowland, **thou** busy sunny river ;
Murmuring once, dimpling, pellucid, limpid, abundant,
  Deepening now, **widening,** swelling, **a lordly river.**
Through woodlands steering, with **branches waving above
    thee,**
  Through the meadows sinuous, wandering irriguous ;
Towns, hamlets leaving, towns by thee, bridges across thee,
  Pass to palace garden, pass to cities populous.
Murmuring once, dimpling, 'mid woodlands **wandering idly,**
Tow with mighty vessels loaded, a mighty river.
Pass to the great waters, though tides may seem **to resist thee ;**
  Tides to resist seeming, quickly will lend thee passage,
Pass to the dark waters that roaring wait **to receive thee ;**
  Pass them thou **wilt not, thou busy sunny river.**

A. H. CLOUGH.

[*From* Alteram Partem.]

THE rivers flow into the sea
  Is loss and waste, the foolish say,
Nor know that back they find their way,
Unseen, to where they wont to be.

A. H. CLOUGH.

[*From* The Spanish Gipsy, Book i.]

RIVERS blent take in a broader heaven.

GEORGE ELIOT

[*From* The Roman, Scene vii.]

NEAR, below, a rushing torrent its long dance of beauty
    led,
And a forest-beast of grandeur cross'd it with a stately tread ;
Golden ran the rapid river gleaming though the skies were
    cold,
Far into the Sabine distance, mantling with its sands of gold.
Said Quirinus, sad, but proudly, gazing with a look sublime,
"Gods ! so fording life, would I send golden sands down
    streams of time !"
He look'd up to heaven, and he look'd down upon the river
    strand :
Smiling through the crystal water, shining lay the un-
    troubled sand.
Said Quirinus, proud, but sadly, gazing upon frith and firth,
"Gods ! so shall the tide of ages rase my footsteps from the
    earth !"

SYDNEY DOBELL.

[*From* The Roman, Scene ix.]

SIRS, where my garden joins the fields
    Low in the vale, no hedge shuts out the fairies,
But Art and Nature, intimately sweet,
Exchange their beauties. Fond amidst them runs
A brook, that like some babbling child between

Two bashful **lovers,** telling tales to each,
Perfects their friendship.   Bowering all the way
With equal joy, they clothe it, **and** in love
Shut out the very sun.

S. DOBELL.

[*From* To the Nile.]

MYSTERIOUS Flood,—that through the silent sands
   Hast wandered, century on century,
Watering the length of great Egyptian lands,
   Which were not, but **for thee,**—

Art thou the keeper of that oldest **lore,**
   Written ere **yet thy** hieroglyphs began,
When dawned upon thy fresh, **untrammeled shore**
   The earliest life of Man?

Thou guardest temple and **vast** pyramid,
   Where the grey Past records its ancient speech;
But **in** thine unrevealing breast lies hid
   What they refuse to teach.

All other streams with human joys and fears
   Run blended, o'er the plains of History;
Thou tak'st no note of Man; a thousand years
   Are as a day to thee.

BAYARD TAYLOR.

Discouraged.

WHERE the little babbling streamlet
   First springs forth to light,
Trickling through soft velvet mosses,
   Almost hid from sight ;
   Vowed I with delight,—
" River, I will follow thee,
Through thy wanderings to the Sea !"

Gleaming 'mid the purple heather,
   Downward then it sped,
Glancing through the mountain gorges,
   Like a silver thread,
   As it quicker-fled,
Louder music in its flow,
Dashing to the vale below.

Then its voice grew lower, gentler,
   And its pace less fleet,
Just as though it loved to linger
   Round the rushes' feet,
   As they stooped to meet
Their clear images below,
Broken by the ripples' flow.

Purple Willow-herb bent over
   To her shadow fair ;
Meadow sweet, in feathery clusters,

Perfumed all the air ;
Silver-weed was there,
And in one calm, grassy spot,
Starry, blue Forget-me-not.

Tangled weeds, below the waters,
Still seemed drawn away ;
Yet the current, floating onward,
Was less strong than they ;—
Sunbeams watched their play,
With a flickering light and shade,
Through the screen the Alders made.

Broader grew the flowing River ;
To its grassy brink
Slowly, in the slanting sun-rays,
Cattle trooped to drink :
The blue sky, I think,
Was no bluer than that stream,
Slipping onward, like a dream.

Quicker, deeper then it hurried,
Rushing fierce and free ;
But I said, " It should grow calmer,
Ere it meets the Sea,
The wide purple Sea,
Which I weary for in vain,
Wasting all my toil and pain."

But it rushed still quicker, fiercer,
In its rocky bed,

Hard and stony was the pathway
 To my tired tread ;
  " I despair," I said,
" Of that wide and glorious Sea
That was promised unto me."

So I turned aside, and wandered
 Through green meadows near,
Far away, among the daisies,
 Far away, for fear
 Lest I still should hear
The loud murmur of its song,
As the River flowed along.

Now I hear it not :—I loiter
 Gaily as before ;
Yet I sometimes think,—and thinking
 Makes my heart so sore,—
 Just a few steps more,
And there might have shone for me,
Blue and infinite, the Sea.
     Adelaide Anne Procter.

[*From* Give.]

SEE the rivers flowing
 Downward to the sea,
Pouring all their treasures
 Bountiful and free—

Yet to help their giving
Hidden springs arise ;
Or, if need be, showers
Feed them from the skies !

A. A. PROCTER.

River of Dart.

RIVER of Dart ! O river of Dart !
Every year thou claimest a heart.
Beautiful river, through fringe of fern
Gliding swift to the southern sea,
Such is the fame thy wild waves earn,
Such is the dirge men sing by thee :
For the cry of Dart is the voice of doom,
When the floods are out in the moorland gloom.

River of Dart ! beside thy stream
In the sweet Devon summer I linger and dream ;
For thy mystic pools are dark and deep,
And thy flying waters strangely clear,
And the crags are wild by the Lover's Leap,
And thy song of sorrow I will not hear,
While the fierce moor-falcon floats aloft,
And I gaze on eyes that are loving and soft.

River of Dart ! the praise be thine
For the loving eyes that are meeting mine !

Where thy swift trout leap, and thy swallows dip,
   'Neath a gray tor's shadow 'twas mine to know
The pure first touch of a virgin lip,
   And the virgin pant of a breast of snow.
River of Dart! O river of Dart!
By thy waters wild I have found a heart.

MORTIMER COLLINS.

[*From* The Two Streams.]

THERE have been brotherhoods in song,
   And human friendships true;
There have been lovers unto death,
Yes, and right many too.
But never in the march of time,
And ne'er in mortal knowing,
From history or nobler rhyme
Hath there been such constant flowing:
One from mountains far away,
One from glades of emerald shining,
Flowing, flowing evermore
For a delicate combining.
If upon a summer's day,
When the air is blue and bracing,
You for Merkland take your way,
Sweet uneasy fancies chasing;
You may see the famous grove—
If not famous, then most surely

Ripe for fame, which is but love—
Where they mingle most demurely.
Not in song and babbling play
Which no poet could unravel ;
But in tender simple way,
On a bed of golden gravel.
Where I sit I see them now,—
Bothlin with her endless winding
From a mountain's purple brow,
Sacred contemplation finding;
In still nooks of shady rest,
Gleaming greenly 'neath the holly :
Youth, she says, is often blest
With a touch of melancholy.
Luggie from the oriend fields
Wiser is, yet hath a beauty,
Which the snowy conscience yields
To the softened face of duty.
All she does bespeaks a grace,
Yet the grace hath that of sadness.
We behold in many a face,
Where we had expected gladness.
But when Bothlin meets her there,
See the change to sudden glory !
Surely such another pair
Never met in classic story.

DAVID GRAY.

The Brooklet.

O DEEP unlovely brooklet, moaning slow
   Thro' moorish fen in utter loneliness !
The partridge cowers beside thy loamy flow
   In pulseful tremor, when with sudden press
The huntsman flusters thro' the rustled heather.
   In March thy sallow-buds from vermeil shells
Break, satin-tinted, downy as the feather
   Of moss-chat that among the purplish bells
Breasts into fresh new life her three unborn.
   The plover hovers o'er thee, uttering clear
And mournful-strange, his human cry forlorn :
   While wearily, alone, and void of cheer
Thou glid'st thy nameless waters from the fen,
To sleep unsunned in an untrampled glen.

D. GRAY.

[*From* The Luggie.]

B ETWEEN its spotless-clothëd banks, in clear
   Pellucid luculence, the Luggie seems
Charmed in its course, and with deceptive calm
Flows mazily in unapparent lapse,
A liquid silence.

D. GRAY.

[*From* The Luggie.]

OVER the mill dam
  Sounding, **a cataract in** miniature,
White-robed it dashes thro' **unceasing mist.**
Thro' ivied bridge, adown **its rocky bed**
Shadowed by **wavy limes whose branches bend**
Kissing the wave to ripples, **on it** purls
Abrupt, capricious, past the hazel bower
Where marriageable maid is being **woo'd.**

D. GRAY.

[*From* Colibri, Canto iii.]

AND now the waters **dream**
  And darken in the **shadows where they keep**
Rich stains of leaf and flower buried deep,
In pastures where the feeding fishes gleam,
Spangled with sun and stars ; and now the stream,
Bounding with glossy back beneath some cape,
Goes onward like an oscillating snake,
Until one midmost rock's unyielding shape
Thwarts it, and lo ! whole **seas** of fury break
From lashed sides, and the rock and river **wage**
A roaring, endless strife.

ARTHUR O'SHAUGHNESSY.

[*From* At Stratford-upon-Avon.]

AND, touched with the sweet glamour of the year,
The winding Avon murmured in its bed.

THOMAS BAILEY ALDRICH.

The Valley Stream.

STREAM flowing swiftly, what music is thine?
The breezy rock-pass, and the storm-wooing pine,
Have taught thee their murmurs,
Their wild mountain murmurs;
Subdued in thy liquid response to a sound
Which aids the repose of this pastoral ground;
Where mingles our valley an awe with the love
It smiles to the sheltering bastions above:
Thy cloud-haunted birthplace,
O Stream, flowing swiftly!

Encircle our meadows with bounty and grace;
Then move on thy journey with tranquiller pace,
To find the great waters,
The great ocean-waters,
Blue, wonderful, boundless to vision or thought;—
Thence, thence, might thy musical tidings be brought!
One waft of the tones of the infinite sea!
Our gain is but songs of the mountain from thee,
O child of the mountain!
O Stream of our Valley!

And have we divined what is thunder'd and hiss'd,
Where the lofty ledge glimmers through screens of gray mist,
    And raves forth its secrets,
    The heart of its secrets?
Or learn'd what is hid in thy whispering note,
Mysteriously gather'd from fountains remote,
To the peak and the fell?   O what music is thine
Thou swift-flowing River, if soul's ear be fine,
    Far-wafted, prophetic,
    Thou Stream of our Valley!

WILLIAM ALLINGHAM.

Æolian Harp.

WHAT saith the river to the rushes gray,
    Rushes sadly bending,
   River slowly wending?
Who can tell the whisper'd things they say?
    Youth, and prime, and life, and time,
    For ever, ever fled away!

Drop your wither'd garlands in the stream,
    Low autumnal branches,
    Round the skiff that launches
Wavering downward through the lands of dream.
    Ever, ever fled away!
    This the burden, this the theme.

What saith the river to the rushes gray,
    Rushes sadly bending
   River slowly wending?

It is near the closing of the day,
　　Near the night.　Life and light
　　For ever, ever fled away !

Draw him tideward down ; but not in haste,
　　Mouldering daylight lingers ;
　　Night with her cold fingers
Sprinkles moonbeams on the dim sea-waste.
　　Ever, ever fled away !
　　Vainly cherish'd ! vainly chased !

What saith the river to the rushes gray,
　　Rushes sadly bending
　　River slowly wending ?
Where in darkest glooms his bed we lay,
　　Up the cave moans the wave,
　　For ever, ever, ever fled away !

W. ALLINGHAM.

The Rhine and the Moselle.

A S the glory of the sun,
　　When the dismal night is done,
Leaps upward in the summer-blue to shine,
　　So gloriously flows
　　From his cradle in the snows
The king of all the river floods—the Rhine.

As a mailed and sceptred king
Sweeps onwards triumphing,
With waves of helmets flashing in his line,
As a drinker past control
With the red wine on his soul,
So flashes through his vintages—the Rhine.

As a lady who would speak
What is written on her cheek,
If her heart would give her tongue the leave to tell ;
Who fears and follows still,
And dares not trust her will,
So follows all his windings—the Moselle.

Like the silence that is broken,
When the wished-for word is spoken,
And the heart hath a home where it may dwell ;
Like the sense of sudden bliss,
And the first long loving kiss
Is the meeting of the Rhine and the Moselle.

Like the two lives that are blended
When the loneliness is ended,
The loneliness each heart hath known so well ;
Like the sun and moon together
In a sky of splendid weather,
Is the marriage of the Rhine and the Moselle.

EDWIN ARNOLD.

[*From* The Twelve Months—July.]

QUIET, in the reaches of the river
    Blooms the sea-poppy all alone;
Hidden by the marshy sedges ever,
    Who knows its golden cup is blown?
Who cares if far-distant billows,
    Rocking the great ships to sea,
Underneath the tassels of the willows,
    Rock the sea-poppy and the bee?

                    E. ARNOLD.

[*From* Sohrab and Rustum.]

BUT the majestic river floated on,
    Out of the mist and hum of that low land,
Into the frosty starlight, and there moved,
Rejoicing, through the hush'd Chorasmian waste,
Under the solitary moon;—he flow'd
Right for the polar star, past Orgunjè,
Brimming, and bright, and large; then sands begin
To hem his watery march, and dam his streams,
And split his currents; that for many a league
The shorn and parcell'd Oxus strains along
Through beds of sand and matted rushy isles—
Oxus, forgetting the bright speed he had
In his high mountain cradle in Pamere,
A foil'd circuitous wanderer—till at last

The long'd-for dash of waves is heard, and wide
His luminous home of waters opens, bright
And tranquil, from whose floor the new-bathed stars
Emerge, and shine upon the Aral Sea.

MATTHEW ARNOLD.

[*From* Drifting Down.]

DRIFTING down in the grey-green twilight,
 O, the scent of the new-mown hay !
The oars drip in the mystic shy light,
 O, the charm of the dying day !
While fading flecks of bright opalescence
 But faintly dapple a saffron sky,
The stream flows on with superb quiescence,
 The breeze is hushed to the softest sigh.
 Drifting down in the sweet still weather,
  O, the fragrance of fair July !
 Love, my love, when we drift together,
  O, how fleetly the moments fly !

 Drifting down on the dear old River,
  O, the music that interweaves !
 The ripples run and the sedges shiver,
  O, the song of the lazy leaves !
And far-off sounds—for the night so clear is—
 Awake the echoes of by-gone times ;
The muffled roar of the distant weir is
 Cheered by the clang of the Marlow chimes.

S

Drifting down in the cloudless weather,
  O, how short is the summer day !
Love, my love, when we drift together,
  O, how quickly we drift away !

J. ASHBY-STERRY.

The Brook.

BROOK, happy brook, that glidest through my dell ;
  That trippest with soft feet across the mead ;
That, laughing on, a mazy course dost lead,
O'er pebble beds, and reeds, and rushy swell ;
Go by that cottage where my love doth dwell.
Ripple thy sweetest ripple, sing the best
Of melodies thou hast ; lull her to rest
With such sweet tales as thou dost love to tell
Say, " One is sitting in your wood to-night,
O maiden rare, to catch a glimpse of you ;
A shadow fleet, or but a window-light,
Shall make him glad, and thrill his spirit through."
Brook, happy brook, I pray, go lingering ;
And underneath the rosy lattice sing.

THOMAS ASHE.

[*From* The Human Tragedy, Act i.]

THEN would a freshet runnel cross their track,
  Low-purling to itself for secret bliss,
Now pattering onwards, now half-turning back,

To give the smooth round pebbles one more kiss :
Here travelling straight as haste, there, with changed tack,
Meandering on in utter waywardness.
Now diving under tangled grass, and then
With frolic laugh bubbling to sight again.

ALFRED AUSTIN.

[*From* The Human Tragedy, Act i.]

A RIVER journeyeth past its ancient walls,
    Whereon hoar ivy thrives and night-owls build.
Its only chant is now a waterfall's,
Which swells, and falls, and swells, as it is filled
With music from the hills.   The cuckoo calls
Throughout moist May.   When August woods are stilled
In sleepy sultriness, the stock-dove broods
Low to itself.   The rest is solitude's.

But many a mile before the river sweeps,
With gentle curve, around the Abbey gray,
Straight through dense woods in whose umbrageous deeps
A mystic muteness lurks, it keeps its way.
Now through a throttling gorge it gurgling leaps,
Now flows, slow, smooth, silent as those that pray,
'Twixt sylvan sanctuaries, whose green aisles slope
Up to bare moors, with the bare sky for cope.

A. AUSTIN.

[*From* The Human Tragedy, Act iii.]

THROUGH scarred Chiusa's choked ravine
    Fierce-foaming Dora flows,
Whose sons have ever fearless been
    As its sun-gazing snows.
Past Casentino's fruitful vale
    See smiling Arno glide,
To where fair Florence, famed in tale,
    Glows like a youthful bride.
'Mong green Venafro's olive slopes
    Volturno twists and winds,
And, laughing, triples all the hopes
    Of Capua's happy hinds.
'Tis only Tiber—Tiber—crawls,
    Sullen from swamp to sea.

A. AUSTIN.

[*From* The Glories of our Thames.]

O MANY a river song has sung and dearer made the
    names
Of Tweed and Ayr and Nith and Doon, but who has
    sung our Thames?
And much green Kent and Oxfordshire and Middlesex it
    shames
That they've not given long since one song to their own
    noble Thames.

O clear are England's waters all, her rivers, streams and
    rills,
Flowing stilly through her valleys lone and winding up her
    hills,
But river, stream, or rivulet through all her breadth who
    names
For beauty and for pleasantness with our own pleasant
    Thames.

The men of grassy Devonshire the Tamar well may love,
And well may rocky Derbyshire be noisy of her Dove,
But with all their grassy beauty, nor Dove nor Tamar
    shames,
Nor Wye, beneath her winding woods, our own green
    pleasant Thames.

I care not if it rises in the Seven Wells' grassy springs,
Or at Thanes' head whence the rushy Churn its gleaming
    waters brings,
From the Cotswolds to the heaving Nore, our praise and
    love it claims,
From the Isis' fount to the salt sea Nore, how pleasant is
    the Thames !

O Gloucestershire and Wiltshire well its gleaming waters
    love,
And Oxfordshire and Berkshire rank it all their streams
    above ;
Nor Middlesex nor Essex nor Kent nor Surrey claims
A river equal in their love to their own noble Thames.

How many a brimming river swells its waters deep and clear,
The Windrush and the Cherwell and the Thame to Dorset
    dear,
The Kennet and the Lodden that have music in their names,
But no grandeur like to that in yours, my own mast-shadow'd
    Thames.

.   .   .   .

Flow on in glory, still flow on, O Thames, unto the sea,
Through glories gone, through grandeurs here, through
    greatness still to be :
Through the free homes of England flow, and may yet
    higher fames,
Still nobler glories star your course, O my own native
    Thames !

WILLIAM COX BENNET.

[*From* Mudal in June.]

MUDAL, that comes from the lonely mere,
    Silent or whispering, vanishing ever,
Know you of aught that concerns us here ?—
    You, youngest of all God's creatures, a river.

Born of a yesterday's summer shower,
    And hurrying on with your restless motion,
Silent or whispering, every hour,
    To lose yourself in the great lone ocean.

Your banks remain ; but you go by,
    Through day and through darkness swiftly sailing ;

Say, do you hear the curlew cry,
  And the snipe in the night-time hoarsely wailing?

Do you watch the wandering hinds in the morn;
  Do you hear the grouse-cock crow in the heather;
Do you see the lark spring up from the corn,
  All in the radiant summer weather?

WILLIAM BLACK.

[*From* Paracelsus.—v.]

*F*ESTUS. Thus the Mayne glideth
    Where my Love abideth.
Sleep's no softer: it proceeds
On through lawns, on through meads,
On and on, whate'er befall,
Meandering and musical,
Though the niggard pasturage
Bears not on its shaven ledge
Aught but weeds and waving grasses
To view the river as it passes,
Save here and there a scanty patch
Of primroses too faint to catch
A weary bee.
    Paracelsus. More, more; say on!
    Fest.   And scarce it pushes
Its gentle way through strangling rushes,
Where the glossy king-fisher

Flutters when noon-heats are near,
Glad the shelving banks to shun,
Red and streaming in the sun,
Where the shrew-mouse with pale throat
Burrows, and the speckled stoat ;
Where the quick sandpipers flit
In and out the marl and grit
That seems to breed them, brown as they :
Nought disturbs its quiet way,
Save some lazy stork that springs,
Trailing it with legs and wings,
Whom the shy fox from the hill
Rouses, creep he ne'er so still.

ROBERT BROWNING.

[*From* La Saisiaz.]

ASK the rush if it suspects
    Whence and how the stream which floats it had a rise, and where and how
Falls or flows on still ! What answer makes the rush except that now
Certainly it floats and is, and, no less certain than itself,
Is the everyway external stream that now through shoal and shelf
Floats it onward, leaves it—may be—wrecked at last, or lands on shore
There to root again and grow and flourish stable evermore.

—May be ! mere surmise not knowledge : much conjecture
  styled belief,
What the rush conceives the stream means through the
  voyage blind and brief.

BROWNING

[*From* In a Gondola.]

OH, which were best, to roam or rest ?
    The land's lap or the water's breast ?
To sleep on yellow millet-sheaves,
Or swim in lucid shallows, just
Eluding water-lily leaves,
An inch from Death's black fingers, thrust
To lock you, whom release he must ;
Which life were best on Summer eves ?

BROWNING.

[*From* Sordello, Book vi.]

LIKE yonder breadth of watery heaven, a bay,
    And that sky-space of water, ray for ray
And star for star, one richness where they mixed
As this and that wing of an angel, fixed,
Tumultuary splendours folded in
To die.

BROWNING.

[*From* Saul.]

AND the little brooks witnessing murmured, persistent
    and low,
With their obstinate, all but hushed voices—"e'en so, it is so!"

BROWNING.

[*From* Pauline.]

FAR off the river
    Sweeps like a sea, barred out from land; but one—
One thin clear sheet has over-leaped and wound
Into this silent depth, which gained, it lies
Still, as but let by sufferance; the trees bend
O'er it as wild men watch a sleeping girl,
And through their roots long creeping plants stretch out
Their twined hair, steeped and sparkling; farther on,
Tall rushes and thick flag-knots have combined
To narrow it; so, at length, a silver thread,
It winds, all noiselessly through the deep wood
Till thro' a cleft-way, thro' the moss and stone,
It joins its parent-river with a shout.

BROWNING.

Cry of the Little Brook.

CHRIST help me! whither would my dark thoughts run,
    I look around me, trembling fearfully;
The dreadful silence of the Silent One

Freezes my lips, and all is sad to see.
Hark ! hark ! what small voice murmurs
  " God made *me !* "
It is the Brooklet, singing all alone,
Sparkling with pleasure that is all **its own,**
  And running, self-contented, sweet, **and free.**
O **Brooklet,** born where never **grass is green,**
  Finding the stony hill and **flowing fleet,**
Thou **comest as a Messenger serene,**
  With shining wings and silver sandall'd feet ;
Faint falls thy music **on a** Soul unclean,
  And, in a moment, all the World looks sweet !

Robert Buchanan.

[*From* Down the River.]

HOW merry **a life** the little **River leads,**
  Piping a vagrant **ditty free from care ;**
Now rippling as it rushes through the **reeds**
And broad-leaved lilies sailing here and there,
Now lying level with the clover meads
And musing in a mist of silver air !
Bearing a pastoral peace where'er it goes,
Narrow'd to mirth or broaden'd to repose :
Through copsy villages and tiny towns,
By belts of woodland singing sweet,
Pausing where sun and shadow meet
Without the darkness of the breezy downs,

Bickering o'er the keystone as it flows
'Neath mossy bridges arch'd like maiden feet;
And slowly widening as it seaward goes,
Because its summer mission grows complete.

 . . . .

The River, narrow'd to a woody glen,
Leaps trembling o'er a little rocky ledge,
Then broadens forward into calm again
Where the gray moor-hen builds her nest of sedge;
Caught, in the dark those willow-trees have made,
Lipping the yellow lilies o'er and o'er,
It flutters twenty feet along the shade,
Halts at the sunshine like a thing afraid,
And turns to kiss the lilies yet once more.

Those little falls are lurid with the rain
That ere the day is done will come again.
The River falters swoll'n and brown,
Falters, falters, as it nears them,
Shuddering back as if it fears them,
Falters, falters, falters, falters,
Then dizzily rushes down.
But all is calm again, the little River
Smiles on and sings the song it sings for ever.
Here at the curve it passes tilth and farm,
And faintly flowing onward to the mill
It stretches out a little azure arm
To aid the miller, aiding with a will,
And singing, singing still.

R. BUCHANAN.

Loch Leven's Gentle Stream.

I'VE gazed upon the rapid Rhine,
　　I've seen its waters foam and shine;
I've watched its cascades, wild and **bright,**
Leap proudly on, in rainbow **light;**
Its waves have charmed my **dazzled eye,**
Like molten silver clashing by:
Still, still, I could not love the **Rhine;**
The land it watered was not mine:
I sighed **to see the moon's mild beam**
Fall on Loch Leven's gentle stream!

I've wandered by the placid Rhone,
When night was **on her** starry **throne;**
I've **looked** upon **the** Tiber's **tide,**
And **plucked the wild-flowers by its side;**
I've heard **the gondolier's wild note**
O'er the Lagoon's fair waters float:
Still, still, I turned with willing feet,
My native North **again to greet!**
Again to see the **moon's mild beam**
Fall on Loch Leven's gentle stream!

ELIZA COOK.

[*From* The **Thames.**]

LET the Rhine be blue and bright,
　　In its path of liquid light,
Where the red grapes fling **a beam**
Of glory on the stream;

Let the gorgeous beauty there,
Mingle all that's rich and fair;
Yet to me it ne'er could be
Like that river great and free,
        The Thames! the mighty Thames!

Though it bear no azure wave,
Though no pearly foam may lave,
Or leaping cascades pour
Their rainbows on its shore;
Yet I ever loved to dwell
Where I heard its gushing swell;
And never skimmed its breast,
But I warmly praised and blest
        The Thames! the mighty Thames!

                                    E. COOK.

[*From* The Singer's Plea.]

THE ancient rivers, rivers of renown,
    A royal largess to the sea roll down,
And on those liberal highways nations send
Their tributes to the world,—stored corn and wine,
  Gold-dust, the wealth of pearls, and orient spar,
  And myrrh, and ivory, and cinnabar,
  And dyes to make a presence-chamber shine.
But in the woodlands, where the wild flowers are,
  The rivulets, they must have their innocent will
Who all the summer hours are singing still,

The birds care for them, and sometimes a star,
And should a tired child rest beside the stream
Sweet memories would slide into his dream.

       EDWARD DOWDEN.

[*From* Wise Passiveness.]

I LIE as patient as yon wealthy stream,
 Dreaming among green fields its summer dream,
Which takes whate'er the gracious hours will bring
Into its quiet bosom.

       E. DOWDEN.

To the River Clyde.

I.

SWEET stream ! whose infancy is 'mong the hills !
 In joy of youth o'er many a crag thou leapest.
Gladly thou drinkest of a hundred rills,
Till growing strong thy seaward tryst thou keepest
'Mid farms and orchards is thy pleasant way,
Past wooded slopes, by pale and stately mansions :
Old bridges span thee, and old ruins gray
Are mirror'd in thy still and blue expansions :
Lovely thou art, but natural loveliness
May don a dress demure for deeds of duty :
Drudge of the city ! can I love thee less
That thou art more for use and less for beauty ?
A prouder beauty, my own Clyde ! is thine,
That labour links thee with the mighty brine !

II.

O MIGHTY Clyde ! full-breasted like a sea !
Pure as at bubbling of thy grassy fountains !
Man may not subjugate what God makes free :
Thy plighted ocean-waves, thy glens, thy mountains,
Glow with the colours that our sea-king sires
Pausing beheld amid their tameless forays :
Unchanged the outline of thy rugged shires,
Thy purple slopes, gray headlands, rocky corries,
Sunshine and shattering storms : along thy marge
The far-arm'd city sprinkles rare adornings,
But Nature's features, unsubdued and large,
Keep their old pomp as in the primal mornings,
When first with thee I dreamt delirious dreams,
Thou peerless daughter of the clouds and streams !

        JAMES HEDDERWICK.

[*From* The Hudson.]

" THERE flows a fair stream by the hills of the west,"—
   She sang to her boy as he lay on her breast ;
" Along its smooth margin thy fathers have played ;
Beside its deep waters their ashes are laid."

I wandered afar from the land of my birth,
I saw the old rivers, renowned upon earth,
But fancy still painted that wide-flowing stream
With the many-hued pencil of infancy's dream.

I saw the green banks of the castle-crowned Rhine,
Where the grapes drink the moonlight and change it to wine;
I stood by the Avon, whose waves as they glide
Still whisper his glory who sleeps **at their side.**

But my heart would still **yearn for the sound of the waves**
That sing as they **flow by** my forefathers' graves ;
If manhood **yet** honours my cheek with a tear,
I care not who sees it,—no blush for it here !

OLIVER WENDELL HOLMES.

Little Streams.

LITTLE streams in **light and shadow,**
  Flowing through **the pasture meadow,**
Flowing by the green **way-side,**
Through the forest dim and **wide,**
Through the hamlet still and **small—**
By the cottage, by the hall,
By the ruin'd abbey still ;
Turning here and there **a** mill,
Bearing tribute to the river—
Little streams, I love you ever.

Summer music there is flowing—
Flowering plants in them are growing ;
Happy life is in them all,
Creatures innocent and small ;
Little birds come down to drink,
Fearless of their leafy brink ;

Noble trees beside them grow,
Glooming them with branches low ;
And between, the sunshine, glancing,
In their little waves, is dancing.

Little streams have flowers a many,
Beautiful and fair as any ;
Typha strong, and green bur-reed ;
Willow-herb, with cotton-seed ;
Arrow-head, with eye of jet ;
And the water-violet.
There the flowering-rush you meet,
And the plumy meadow-sweet ;
And, in places deep and stilly,
Marble-like, the water-lily.

Little streams, their voices cheery,
Sound forth welcomes to the weary,
Flowing on from day to day,
Without stint and without stay ;
Here, upon their flowery bank,
In the old time pilgrims drank—
Here have seen, as now, pass by,
King-fisher, and dragon-fly ;
Those bright things that have their dwelling,
Where the little streams are welling.

Down in valleys green and lowly,
Murmuring not and gliding slowly ;

Up in mountain-hollows wild,
Fretting like a peevish child;
Through the hamlet, where all day
In their waves the children play;
Running west, **or running east,**
Doing good to man and beast—
Always giving, weary never,
Little streams, **I love you ever.**

MARY HOWITT

[*From* Divided.]

WE two walk till the purple dieth
    And short dry grass under foot is brown;
But one little streak **at a distance lieth**
    Green like **a ribbon to prank the down.**

.   .   .

Hey the green ribbon! we kneeled beside it,
    We parted the grasses dewy and sheen;
Drop over drop there filtered and slided
    A tiny bright beck that trickled between.

. . . . . .

A dappled sky, a world of meadows,
    Circling above us the black rooks fly
Forward, backward; lo, their dark shadows
    Flit **on** the blossoming tapestry—

Flit on the beck, for her long grass parteth
    As hair from a maid's bright eyes blown back ;
And, lo, the sun like a lover darteth
    His flattering smile on her wayward track.

  .   .   .   .

A breathing sigh, a sigh for answer,
    A little talking of outward things :
The careless beck is a merry dancer,
    Keeping sweet time to the air she sings.

A little pain when the beck grows wider;
    " Cross to me now—for her wavelets swell : "
" I may not cross "—and the voice beside her
    Faintly reacheth, though heeded well.

  .   .   .   .   .   .

A rose-flush tender, a thrill, a quiver,
    When golden gleams to the tree-tops glide ;
A flashing edge for the milk-white river,
    The beck, a river—with still sleek tide.

Broad and white, and polished as silver,
    On she goes under fruit-laden trees :
Sunk in leafage cooeth the culver,
    And 'plaineth of love's disloyalties,

  .   .   .   .   .   .

A braver swell, a swifter sliding ;
    The river hasteth, her banks recede :
Wing-like sails on her bosom gliding,
    Bear down the lily and drown the reed.

Stately prows are rising and bowing
  (Shouts of mariners winnow the air),
And level sands for banks endowing
  The tiny green ribbon that showed so fair.
JEAN INGELOW.

[*From* The Letter L.]

THE happy wave ran up and rang
  Like service bells a long way off,
And down a little freshet sprang
  From mossy trough,

And splashed into a rain of spray,
  And fretted on with daylight's loss,
Because so many bluebells lay
  Leaning across.
JEAN INGELOW.

[*From* The Letter L.]

THE busy beck, that still would run
  And fall, and falter its refrain ;
And pause and shimmer in the sun,
  And fall again.

It led me to the sandy shore,
  We sang together, it and I—
"The daylight comes, and dark is o'er,
  The shadows fly."
JEAN INGELOW.

[*From* Gladys and Her Island.]

RIVERS shall run on,
Full of sweet language as a lover's mouth.

JEAN INGELOW.

[*From* Thames.]

A GLIMPSE of the river! it glimmers
Through the stems of the beeches;
Through the screen of the willows it shimmers
In long winding reaches;
Flowing so softly that scarcely
It seems to be flowing,
But the reeds of the low little islands
Are bent to its going;
And soft as the breath of a sleeper
Its heaving and sighing,
In the coves where the fleets of the lilies
At anchor are lying:
It looks as if fallen asleep
In the lap of the meadows, and smiling
Like a child in the grass, dreaming deep
Of the flowers and their golden beguiling.

ISABELLA CRAIG KNOX.

Ballade of the Tweed.

THE ferox rins in rough Loch Awe,
    A weary cry frae ony toun ;
The Spey, that loups o'er linn and fa',
They praise a' ither streams aboon ;
They boast their braes o' bonny Doon :
Gie *me* to hear the ringing reel,
Where shilfas sing and cushats croon,
By fair Tweed-side, at Ashiesteel !

There's Ettrick, Meggat, Ail, and a',
Where trout swim thick in May and June ;
Ye'll see them take in showers o' snaw
Some blinking, cauldrife April noon :
Rax ower the palmer and march-broun,
And syne we'll show a bonny creel,
In spring or simmer, late or soon,
By fair Tweed-side, at Ashiesteel !

There's mony a water, great or sma',
Gaes singing in his siller tune,
Through glen and heugh, and hope and shaw,
Beneath the sun-licht or the moon :
But set us in our fishing-shoon
Between the Caddon-burn and Peel,
And syne we'll cross the heather broun
By fair Tweed-side, at Ashiesteel !

ENVOY.

Deil take the dirty, trading loon
Wad gar the water ca' his wheel,
And drift his dyes and poisons doun
By fair Tweed-side, at Ashiesteel !

ANDREW LANG.

[*From* The Last Cast.]

BRIEF are men's days at best ; perchance
    I waste my own, who have not seen
The castled palaces of France
    Shine on the Loire in summer green.

And clear and fleet Eurotas still,
    You tell me, laves his reedy shore,
And flows beneath his fabled hill
    Where Dian drave the chase of yore.

And " like a horse unbroken " yet
    The yellow stream with rush and foam,
'Neath tower, and bridge, and parapet,
    Girdles his ancient mistress, Rome !

I may not see them, but I doubt,
    If seen I'd find them half so fair
As ripples of the rising trout
    That feed beneath the elms of Yair.

Nay, Spring I'd meet by Tweed or Ail,
   And Summer by Loch Assynt's deep,
And Autumn in that lonely vale
   Where wedded Avons westward sweep.

Or where, amid the empty fields,
   Among the bracken of the glen,
Her yellow wreath October yields,
   To crown the crystal brows of Ken.

A. Lang.

[*From* Beaver Brook.]

WARM noon brims full the valley's cup,
   The aspen's leaves are scarce astir;
Only the little mill sends up
Its busy, never-ceasing burr. . . .

No mountain torrent's strength is here;
Sweet Beaver, child of forest still,
Heaps its small pitcher to the ear,
And gently waits the miller's will.

Swift slips Undine along the race
Unheard, and then, with flashing bound,
Floods the dull wheel with light and grace,
And, laughing, hunts the loath drudge round.

The miller dreams not at what cost
The quivering mill stones hum and whirl,

Nor how for every turn are tost
Armfuls of diamond and of pearl.

But Summer cleared my happier eyes
With drops of some celestial juice,
To see how Beauty underlies
Forevermore each form of Use.

And more : methought I saw that flood,
Which now so dull and darkling steals,
Thick, here and there, with human blood,
To turn the world's laborious wheels.

No more than doth the miller there,
Shut in our various cells, do we
Know with what waste of beauty rare
Moves every day's machinery.

JAMES RUSSELL LOWELL.

[*From* Songs of the Summer Nights, ii.]

MY boat glides with the gliding stream,
　　Following adown its breast
One flowing mirrored amber gleam,
　　The death-smile of the west.

The river flows : the sky is still ;
　　No ceaseless quest it knows :
Thy bosom swells, thy fair eyes fill
　　At sight of such repose.

The ripples flow : unmoving sit
The stars above the night,
In shade and gleam the waters flit :
Yon pearly path, how bright !

GEORGE MACDONALD.

[*From* The Water Tarantella.]

THE wind blows low on the fields and hedges,
There is a murmur amid the sedges,
A low sweet sound where the water gushes
Forth from the grass amid the rushes ;
It is a streamlet small and young,
It loves to dally the mosses among,
It trickles slowly,
It whispers lowly,
On its breast the thistle drops its down,
The water-lily
So white and stilly
Sleeps in its lap till its leaves grow brown.

.   .   .   .

We will follow thee where it flows --
It leaves the sedges dank behind,
And on its fringe a willow shows
Its silvery leaflets to the wind ;
And a brook comes down from far away,
And babbles into it all the day ;
And both together creep through meads
Where the shy plover hides and feeds,

And then away through fields of corn,
Or stretch of meadows newly shorn :
Noiselessly they flow and clear
By open wold and cover'd brake ;
But if you listen, you may hear
The steady music which they make.

　.　　.　　.　　.　　.　　.

And now the stream begins to run
Over the pebbles in its bed,
To rumple its breast and glance in the sun,
And curl to the light breeze overhead.
No longer loitering, lingering, calm,
It hurries away o'er the chafing shingle,
Humming a song, singing a psalm,
Through the orchard, down the dingle,
Pools like mirrors adorn its breast,
And there the trout and the minnow rest ;
The ringdove sings in her nest alone
The tender song that love has taught her ;
And the redbreast sits on the boulder-stone,
Washing his plumes in the wimpling water.

　.　　.　　.　　.　　.　　.

Fed by its tributary rills
From distant valleys with circling hills,
And travelling seaward, merrily brawling,
Wild, impassion'd, rapid, and strong,
With voice of power to the green woods calling,
The impetuous river dashes along,
And is sweeping, leaping, through the meadows
Almost as fast as the driving shadows

Of clouds that fly before the wind,
Down to the chasmy precipices,
There to burst in foaming fall ;—
It bursts, it thunders, it roars, it hisses,
An iris is its coronal ;
And the pendulous trees above it shiver,
Bathed by the rain of that rampant river.

. . . . . .

And now the river spends its wrath,
The music sinks, the winds blow low ;
Its bosom broad is a nation's path—
Smooth and pleasant is its flow.
A boat shoots by with its rowers trim,
A ferryman plies his lazy oar ;
And miles adown, in the distance dim,
There stands a city on the shore.

CHARLES MACKAY.

[*From* By the Rosanna.]

THE old grey Alp has caught the cloud,
    And the torrent river sings aloud ;
The glacier-green Rosanna sings
An organ song of its upper springs.
Foaming under the tiers of pine,
I see it dash down the dark ravine,
And it tumbles the rocks in boisterous play,
With an earnest will to find its way.
Sharp it throws out an emerald shoulder,
    And, thundering ever of the mountain,

Slaps in sport some giant boulder,
　　And tops it in a silver fountain.

A chain of foam from end to end,
And a solitude so deep, my friend,
You may forget that man abides
Beyond the great mute mountain-sides.
Yet to me, in this high-walled solitude
Of river and rock and forest rude,
The roaring voice through the long white chain,
Is the voice of the world of bubble and brain.

.　　　.　　　.　　　.　　　.　　　.　　　.

Yea, letting alone the roar and the strife,
This On-on-on is so like life !
Here's devil take the hindmost, too ;
And an amorous wave has a beauty in view ;
And lips of others are kissing the rocks :
Here's chasing of bubbles, and wooing of blocks.
And through the resonant monotone
　I catch wild laughter mix'd with shrieks ;
And a wretched creature's stifled moan,
　Whom Time, the terrible usurer, tweaks.

GEORGE MEREDITH.

[*From* A Yorkshire River.]

THE silent surfaces sleep
　　With a sullen viscous flow,
And scarce in the squalid deep
Swing the dead weeds to and fro,

And no living thing is there to swim or creep
In the sunless gulfs below.

And beneath are the ooze and the slime,
Where the corpse lies as it fell,
The hidden secrets of crime
Which no living tongue shall tell,
The shameful story of time,
The old, old burden of hell.

All the grasses upon the bank
Are bitter with scurf and drift,
And the reeds are withered and dank ;
And sometimes, when the smoke clouds shift,
You may see the tall shafts in a hideous rank
Their sulphurous fumes uplift.

From the black blot up the stream
The funeral barges glide,
And the waves part as in a dream,
From broad bow and sunken side ;
And 'tis "greed, greed!" hisses from coal and from stream,
Foul freightage and turbid tide.

LEWIS MORRIS.

[*From* A Song at a Waterfall.]

ATHWART the voice of a wild water,
    Falling for ever,
Do I hear some song of the foam's daughter
    Fairily quiver ?

Is it song of naiad, or bee,
Or a breeze from the tree,
Haunting the cave of the wild water?

For evermore leapeth the fall plashing
  Into a pool,
And nigh me, away from the foam flashing,
  Quiet and cool
Lies a hyaline gulf olive-green,
Where ferns overlean,
And boughs embower the wave washing.

In a clear hyaline, lo ! the leaves waver,
  While, as a cloud,
Stones below melt in the pool-quaver :
  And with a loud
Shout of the waters blithe
Mingles, airy and lithe,
A tune, like a lingering flower-savour.

      HON. RODEN NOEL.

In the Valley of the Grande Chartreuse.

TORRENT under lofty beeches, under larches cresting
  high,
Wanderer by the wandering stranger slipping softly, surely, by:

Born among Savoyan snows, and where Saint Bruno, hid
  with God,
Far from kindly human love, the road of tears and rapture
  trod :

Joining then the valley-streamlet, then the golden-green
    Isère,
Then, where Rhone's broad currents to the blue their lordly
    burden bear :

—Torrent under lofty beeches, under larches cresting high,
Thou art southward set, and southward all thy waters strain
    and fly :—

Sunny South,—o'er slope and summit the gray mist of olive
    spread ;
Terrace high o'er terrace climbing, lines of white, vine-
    garlanded :

—Ah, another vision calls me, calls me to the northern isle,
Voices from beyond the mountain : smiles that dim the
    sun's own smile :

And I set my soul against thee, water of the southern sea :
—Thine are not the currents toward the haven where my
    heart would be.

FRANCIS TURNER PALGRAVE.

[*From* The Wanderer of Clova.]

FAR from the stir of men
    Lies Clova's lonely glen,
Tracked by the grey South Esk meandering tow'rds the seas;
    On either hand are seen
    Vast walls of living green,
Spotted with crags that mar their verdant harmonies.

U

And where the winter sun,
His short day's journey done,
Behind Tombine's mass betakes him to the night,—
Thence started on its course,
White-Water brings its force
To meet the half-grown Esk in rivalry of might.

Adown the deep Glen Dole
Its foamy torrents roll,
With speed that scarce will grant a moment's breathing
pause,—
Still writhing at the stir
Of terror's urgent spur,
Escaping from the gripe of Luncart's rock-fanged jaws.

But ere the river raves
Through those terrific graves,
It walks with gentler step down lengths of silent vale ;
A place most desolate,
High, bare, flat, formless, straight,—
All black and pallid green, hued like a dragon's mail.

EARL OF SOUTHESK.

[*From* He or She; or, a Poet's Portfolio.]

AFLOAT on the brim of a placid stream,
Pleasant it is to lie and dream,
With heaven above, and far below
The deeps of death—sad deeps that know

The still reflections of earth and sky
In their silent, serene obscurity.
And hanging thus upon Life's thin rim,
Death seems so sweet in that silvery, dim,
Deep world below, that it seems half-best
To sink into it and there find rest,
Both, both together, ere age can come,
And loving has lost its perfect bloom.
One tilt, dear love, and we both might be
Beyond earth's sorrows eternally.

WILLIAM WETMORE STORY.

[*From* Cleopatra.]

THERE, drowsing in golden sunlight,
   Loiters the slow smooth Nile,
Through slender papyri, that cover
   The wary crocodile.
The lotus lolls on the water,
   And opens its heart of gold,
And over its broad leaf-pavement
   Never a ripple is rolled.

W. W. STORY.

[*From* The Triumph of Time.]

THE stream,
   One loose thin pulseless tremulous vein,
Rapid and vivid and dumb as a dream.

ALGERNON CHARLES SWINBURNE.

The Brook.

" I COME from haunts of coot and hern,
  I make a sudden sally,
And sparkle out among the fern,
  To bicker down a valley.

" By thirty hills I hurry down,
  Or slip between the ridges,
By twenty thorps, a little town,
  And half a hundred bridges.

" Till last by Philip's farm I flow
  To join the brimming river,
For men may come and men may go,
  But I go on for ever.

" I chatter over stony ways,
  In little sharps and trebles,
I bubble into eddying bays,
  I babble on the pebbles.

" With many a curve my bank I fret
  By many a field and fallow,
And many a fairy foreland set
  With willow-weed and mallow.

" I chatter, chatter, as I flow
  To join the brimming river,
For men may come and men may go,
  But I go on for ever.

" I wind about, and in and out,
  With here a blossom sailing,
And here and there a lusty trout,
  And here and there a grayling.

" And here and there a foamy flake
  Upon me, as I travel
With many a silvery waterbreak
  Above the golden gravel,

" And draw them all along, and flow
  To join the brimming river,
For men may come and men may go,
  But I go on for ever.

" I steal by lawns and grassy plots,
  I slide by hazel covers ;
I move the sweet forget-me-nots
  That grow for happy lovers.

" I slip, I slide, I gloom, I glance,
  Among my skimming swallows ;
I make the netted sunbeam dance
  Against my sandy shallows.

" I murmur under moon and stars
  In brambly wildernesses ;
I linger by my shingly bars ;
  I loiter round my cresses ;

"And out again I curve and flow
　To join the brimming river,
For men may come and men may go,
　But I go on for ever."

　　　　　　　　ALFRED, LORD TENNYSON.

[*From* Aylmer's Field.]

THE brook
　　Vocal, with here and there a silence, ran
By sallowy rims.

　　　　　　　　LORD TENNYSON.

[*From* A Farewell.]

FLOW down, cold rivulet, to the sea,
　　Thy tribute wave deliver:
No more by thee my steps shall be,
　For ever and for ever.

Flow, softly flow, by lawn and lea,
　A rivulet then a river:
No where by thee my steps shall be,
　For ever and for ever.

　　　　　　　　LORD TENNYSON.

[*From* In Memoriam, xix.]

THE Danube to the Severn gave
   The darken'd heart that beat no more;
   They laid him by the pleasant shore,
And in the hearing of the wave.

There twice a day the Severn fills;
   The salt sea-water passes by,
   And hushes half the babbling Wye,
And makes a silence in the hills.

LORD TENNYSON.

[*From* In Memoriam, xxxv.]

THE sound of streams that swift or slow
   Draw down Æonian hills, and sow
The dust of continents to be.

LORD TENNYSON.

[*From* Œnone.]

FAR below them roars
   The long brook falling thro' the clov'n ravine
In cataract after cataract to the sea.

LORD TENNYSON.

[*From* Ode to Memory.]

THE brook that loves
　　To purl o'er matted crest and ribbed sand,
Or dimple in the dark of rushy coves,
Drawing into his narrow earthen urn,
　　In every elbow and turn,
The filter'd tribute of the rough woodland.

　　　　　　　　　　　LORD TENNYSON.

[*From* The Gardener's Daughter.]

A LEAGUE of grass, wash'd by a slow broad stream,
　　That, stirr'd with languid pulses of the oar,
Waves all its lazy lilies, and creeps on,
Barge-laden, to three arches of a bridge
Crown'd with the minster-towers.

　　　　　　　　　　　LORD TENNYSON.

[*From* The Lotus-Eaters.]

AND like a downward smoke, the slender stream
　　Along the cliff to fall and pause and fall did seem.

　　　　　　　　　　　LORD TENNYSON.

[*From* The Lotus-Eaters.]

A LAND of streams ! some, like a downward smoke
    Slow-dropping veils of thinnest lawn, did go ;
And some thro' wavering lights and shadows broke,
Rolling a slumbrous sheet of foam below.

LORD TENNYSON.

[*From* The Lotus-Eaters.]

BENEATH a heaven dark and holy,
    To watch the long bright river drawing slowly
His waters from the purple hill. . . .
To watch the emerald-colour'd water falling
Thro' many a wov'n acanthus-wreath divine !
Only to hear and see the far-off sparkling brine,
Only to hear were sweet, stretch'd out beneath the pine.

LORD TENNYSON.

[*From* Sonnet.]

THROUGH yonder poplar valley
    Below the blue-green river windeth slowly ;
But in the middle of the sombre valley
The crispèd waters whisper musically.

LORD TENNYSON.

To the Thames.

R IVER, whose charge is from the winds and sky
      The Imperial City's agitated ear
To soothe with murmur low and ceaseless cheer,
Do thy great, pious task perpetually :
But add a warning voice more deep and high :
Borne down from bridge to bridge in smooth career,
Tell her to whom the pomp of gold is dear,
Of Tyre that fell ; of Fortune's perfidy !
Tell her, whilst on thy broad and glimmering mirror
The shadows of her turrets tremble and slide,
How brief the impress of victorious Pride,
How nearly Triumph is allied to Terror.
Demons their nests in ship-mast forests hide—
By nobleness, not gold, are Nations deified.

                                  AUBREY DE VERE.

The Stars in the River.

T HE mirrored stars lit all the bulrush spears,
      And all the flags and broad-leaved lily-isles ;
   The ripples shook the stars to golden smiles,
Then smoothed them back to happy golden spheres.
We rowed—we sang ; her voice seemed, in mine ears,
   An angel's, yet with woman's dearest wiles ;
   But shadows fell from gathering cloudy piles,
And ripples shook the stars to fiery tears.

God shaped **the** shadows like a phantom boat
  Where sate her soul and mine in Doom's attire ;
Along the lily isles **I saw** it **float**
  Where ripples shook the stars to **symbols dire** ;
We wept—we kissed, while starry fingers wrote,
  And ripples shook the **stars to a snake of fire.**

THEODORE WATTS.

[*From* The Auspicious Day.]

Water Nymph's Song.

MILES and miles of here and there
    Our eager river forced its **way,**
Bent to be it knew **not where.**

It **had** no rest in delay ;
  And for its haste it **had no aim** ;
Wherefore go ?   But wherefore stay ?

Here and there **led both the same** ;
  By **any** winding it could make
Near its secret goal it **came.**

When it reached the crystal lake
  It knew its aim and found its rest ;
All the miles were for love's sake.

'Mid the blue hills of the west,
Our river lies **in the** lake's breast.

AUGUSTA WEBSTER.

The Brook Rhine.

SMALL current of the wilds afar from men,
  Changing and sudden as a baby's mood ;
  Now a green babbling rivulet in the wood,
Now loitering broad and shallow through the glen,
Or threading 'mid the naked shoals, and then
  Brattling against the stones, half mist, half flood,
  Between the mountains where the storm-clouds brood ;
And each change but to wake or sleep again ;
  Pass on, young stream, the world has need of thee ;
Far hence a mighty river on its breast
  Bears the deep-laden vessels to the sea ;
Far hence wide waters feed the vines and corn.
Pass on, small stream, to so great purpose born,
  On to the distant toil, the distant rest.

A. WEBSTER.

The Frozen River.

DEAD stream beneath the icy silent blocks
  That motionless stand soddening into grime,
Thy fretted falls hang numb, frost pens the locks ;
  Dead river, when shall be thy waking time ?
"Not dead ;" the river spoke and answered me,
" My burdened current, hidden, finds the sea."
  "Not dead, not dead ;" my heart replied at length,
  "The frozen river holds a hidden strength."

A. WEBSTER.

[*From* Our River.]

The Merrimack.

WE know the world is rich with streams
    Renowned in song and story,
Whose music murmurs through our dreams
    Of human **love** and glory :
We know that Arno's banks are fair,
    And Rhine **has** castled shadows,
And, poet-tuned, **the Doon and Ayr**
    Go singing **down their meadows.**

But while, unpictured and unsung
    By painter or by poet,
Our river waits the tuneful **tongue**
    And cunning **hand to** show **it,**—
We only **know** the fond skies lean
    Above it, **warm with** blessing,
And the sweet soul of our Undine
    Awakes **to our** caressing.

No fickle sun-god holds the flocks
    That graze its shores in keeping ;
No icy kiss of Dion mocks
    The youth beside it sleeping :
Our Christian river loveth most
    The beautiful and human ;
The heathen streams of Naiads **boast,**
    But ours of man and woman.

The miner in his cabin hears
    The ripple we are hearing;
It whispers soft to home-sick ears
    Around the settler's clearing:
In Sacramento's vales of corn,
    Or Santee's bloom of cotton,
Our river by its valley-born,
    Was never yet forgotten.

JOHN GREENLEAF WHITTIER.

INDEX OF WRITERS.

[Those to whose name no date is attached are living writers.]

Falconer, William (1730-1769), 15.
Fletcher, John (1576-1625), 182, 183.

Gay, John (1688-1732), 12.
Gray, David (1838-1861), 264, 266, 267

Hallam, Arthur Henry (1811-1833), 75.
Harte, Bret, 108.
Heber, Reginald (1783-1826), 33.
Hedderwick, James, 108, 109, 287.
Hemans, Felicia Dorothea (1794-1835), 43, 44, 46, 47, 234.
Herrick, Robert (1591-1674), 6, 185, 186.
Hogg, James (1772-1835), 30.
Holmes, Oliver Wendell, 288.
Hopkins, Ellice, 109.
Houghton, Richard, Lord (1809-1885), 75, 76, 254.
Howitt, Mary, 289.
Hunt, Leigh (1784-1859), 219.

Ingelow, Jean, 111, 112, 113, 114, 291, 293, 294.

Keats, John (1796-1821), 50, 235, 236.
Keble, John (1792-1866), 42.
Kingsley, Charles (1819-1875), 79, 80, 255.
Knox, Isa Craig, 294.

Landon, Letitia Elizabeth (1802-1838), 61, 244.
Lang, Andrew, 114.
Longfellow, Henry Wadsworth (1807-1883), 66, 67, 68, 69, 70, 71, 72, 246, 247, 249, 251, 252.
Lover, Samuel (1797-1868), 53.
Lowell, James Russell, 114.

Turnbull & Spears, Printers, Edinburgh.

9 783744 765336